A Beth-Hill Novel:
Karen Montgomery Series Book 2:
The Secret of Redemption

By Jennifer St. Clair

Writers Exchange E-Publishing
http://www.writers-exchange.com

A Beth-Hill Novella: Karen Montgomery Series, Book 2: The Secret of Redemption

Copyright 2007, 2015, 2023 Jennifer St. Clair

Writers Exchange E-Publishing

PO Box 372

ATHERTON QLD 4883

Cover Art by: Jatin

Published by Writers Exchange E-Publishing

http://www.writers-exchange.com

The Book

"M s. Montgomery?" Penny's voice burst from the intercom on my phone, startling me out of a wonderful daydream that involved a book, a beach, and no reporters.

I jerked upright. "Yes?" Did my voice betray the fact that I'd been asleep?

"There's--someone here to see you," Penny said. Her voice dropped to a whisper. "I think--I think he's blind."

For a moment, my mind went blank as I tried to imagine who my visitor could be. Not a reporter--or at least, not a reporter that I'd seen before. Someone local? A concerned patron who wanted more books in Braille?

"Send him in if you don't think he's a reporter in disguise," I said. "What does he want?"

"He said he wanted to talk to you," Penny said. "And he looks familiar. He might have been at the Christmas party."

The Christmas party. My mind cast back, struggling to remember a blind--

"Oh." My heart leapt. What was *he* doing *here?* "Ask him what his name is before you bring him back."

I heard Penny's voice, distant now, as if she didn't just sit down the hall. "Sir, can I ask your name?"

I didn't hear his reply. His voice was too soft for the microphone to pick up.

Penny picked up the phone again. "He says his name is Malachi."

I would not make a member of the Wild Hunt wait. "I'll be right out."

He stood in the reception area, his sightless eyes fixed on Penny's desk, his hands clasped together, as if in prayer. When he heard my footsteps, he raised his head. I could barely see the scars that ravaged his face. I still didn't know the story behind those scars. Considering my lack of authority concerning the Wild Hunt or any other supernatural person who lived in the county, I doubted I ever would.

"Ms. Montgomery." His voice was just as smooth as his Master's, but I sensed something hidden behind his calm. "I apologize for disturbing you without notice."

"You're not disturbing me," I said. "In fact, I'm delighted to see you. Do you want to come into my office and talk? Is everything okay at home?" With Penny only a few feet away, I had to watch what I said about the Hunt's cave in this world, and their rambling house in Faerie.

Malachi cocked his head. "You are--delighted to see me? Why?"

"Come into my office," I said, keenly aware of Penny's sharp ears. I held out my hand, then realized he couldn't see the gesture. "Do you need to--" How did I phrase an offer of help without sounding facetious? "Do you need my help?"

"If you allow me to touch the back of your arm as we walk, I will be fine," Malachi said. "I can't--I do not know this place." He hesitated. "That's one of the reasons why I came."

I stepped in front of him and turned around, offering him my arm. "I'm right in front of you, then. We don't have far to go."

He was silent until we reached my office, his fingers trailing across the walls here and there to familiarize himself with his surroundings. I noticed that he touched the chair I led him to, swiftly determining its height and width so he would not become off balance when he sat down.

He sat stiffly, as if unused to human furnishings, tense and wary, his face a mask.

"Would you like something to drink? I have tea--"

"No, thank you," Malachi said. "I won't take up much of your time. I came--" His hands clutched the arms of the chair, hard enough to make the old oak creak.

"Did you come here by yourself?" I asked, hoping to put him at ease.

He bristled. "I am not helpless!"

"I didn't think you were," I said. "But I've never seen you without another member of the Hunt." In fact, I'd only seen Malachi three times. Once, in their house when I delivered the invitations to the Christmas party. The second time, at the Christmas party, in human form, just as unhappy as he was now. The third time, in the library with Emle and Eri, almost three weeks ago.

And now, of course--so four times. Math was never my strong suit in school.

Malachi took a deep breath. "I am unused to this," he whispered, but I didn't know what he meant. "And I need--help."

Speaking those words out loud drained much of the tension from his body. He slumped in the chair, shrinking in on himself until he lost much of the otherworldly quality that made the Hunt so--seductive. They were, after all, the *Wild Hunt*. Ancient creatures out of myth and legend.

But like all the stories, once you moved past the myths and legends; once the fairy tale was over and you looked beyond the happily ever after, they became something more. Something vibrant. Alive. Individuals in their own right, with their own wants and desires.

I kept my voice soft. "What kind of help do you need?"

"I feel no pity from you," Malachi said. "And you are a good person. I am not. But I think I would like to be. Now that the Hunt is not bound, now that we are free, I think I would like to learn."

This was the most I'd ever heard him speak. I gaped at him for a moment, unsure how to respond. Why had he chosen *me?* And what was I going to do about it?

"Why aren't you a good person?" And why did I feel like I was interviewing a potential employee? "And bear with me if I ask you a stupid question. I'm still new at this, after all. I *don't* know more than you realize."

He nodded slowly. "You know the stories of the Hunt. You know what we once were."

"I've heard the stories," I said. "Some of them, at least. As much as the Council everyone holds in such high esteem has allowed me to know." Which wasn't much. *Ivy* had told me much more than the Council.

In fact, the press releases about the library's endowment had been Council-approved. But only the Director knew *that.*

"The Council is a necessary evil," Malachi said. "And while I did not agree with their binding, it helped us become what we are now." He hesitated. "Some of those stories--most of those stories hold grains of truth that cower in our darkest memories. I would rather those memories remain in the darkness. Our Master calls us family now, but we still serve him with our lives and loyalty."

We meaning the Hunt, of course. And I had noticed more than once their deference to their Master, even now.

"You said the Hunt was free. But you still serve your Master, so you're not really *free*, are you?"

Malachi's eyes narrowed as he tried to put his thoughts into words. "Free--it depends on whom you ask," he said. "I gave my loyalty to my Master, yes, and he still holds my life in his hands. But we are free enough to make our own decisions now, up to a point. We are allowed to argue. To protest. Before--before, we obeyed without thought or question."

"What happened if you questioned an order before?" I asked. Again, I'd heard stories. Mostly from Ivy, who was *not* at all impartial, and could give an opinion on almost everything. Sometimes I forgot she was older than me by almost thirty years.

Malachi shuddered. "Sometimes we died." He caught his breath, as if the memories had grown too strong for him to bear. "I disobeyed him once. And he almost killed me."

"Is that when you lost your sight?" There wasn't any tactful way to ask. But if Gabriel had blinded him, then why keep him around? What good was a blind Hound to a Wild Hunt?

"No." He did not elaborate. "Gabriel did not blind me. In fact, I expected him to cast me out when he found out I was blind, but he did not."

"I see," I said, but I didn't, not really. Not yet. "But let me get this straight. You think you're a bad person because you obeyed your Master's orders without question? Only, if you had tried to disobey him, he would have killed you?"

"After that first time, I made the choice that I wanted to live," Malachi said. "And people suffered because of my choice. People *died*."

It was an interesting dilemma. But I had no idea why he thought I would be able to help him resolve his guilt, if that was what he truly wanted. I was no priest to absolve him, or grant him redemption. But libraries were often confessionals of sorts, something I'd never understood.

Before I could speak, he continued, the expression on his face tortured now. More memories. How could they sleep with such horrible memories lurking in their minds?

"We spent most of our time with the Hunt as Hounds. And we truly could not disobey--when I am a Hound, I feel compelled to do whatever my Master wishes. But when I am in human form--when I am in human form, I realize what I have done." He shuddered. "Do you understand?"

I thought I did, at least this part of it. "Hounds have no conscience. But when you're in human form, you have one?"

"As a Hound, when we are told to hunt, everything is potential prey." Malachi twisted his hands together. "I am not explaining this well. I'm sorry."

When had I left my job as Assistant Director and become a Psychologist? "What do you need *me* for?" I asked, still unclear about that piece of the puzzle. "You can't change the past, Malachi. I know you know that. And you certainly don't need me to tell you that."

He licked his lips. "Yes, I know that. But how--how do I live with the past?"

"By focusing on the future," I said. "And learning from the past. No matter how hard that might be. You'll never be able to forget what Gabriel forced you to do. You could hate him for it, but I don't see that happening. Instead, you seem to be working together to learn to be a family."

Perhaps I *did* have a chance at being a Psychologist. Or would that be a Psychiatrist? I could always write a bestseller along the lines of *Everything I Ever Needed to Know I Learned in my Local Library*. Which, in essence, was true.

Malachi was silent for a long moment. "And what if I have no resources to focus on the future? What if I have spent the last thousand years blindly obeying my Master, save for that one time? How can I change so swiftly?"

"Well, what do you like to do? Besides hunt for prey?" I hesitated to say 'kill people', even though I knew they had killed many people over the years. And that was the reason why the Council had bound the Hunt a century before.

I knew that much, at least. From somewhere, Ivy had produced a photocopy of a journal written by one of those long-ago Council members, chronicling the Hunt's binding. I had read it a month ago. The photocopy had vanished soon after, and I'd not dared ask her where she had found it. Or stolen it from.

The story of the breaking of that bond was less than a year old. The original binding had been meant to last a century, and the Council had freed the Hunt honorably, thus allowing Gabriel and the Hounds to live as they pleased. Within reason, of course.

I had gotten the impression from more than one person that in the beginning, the supernatural community had waited with bated breath for Gabriel to return to his murdering ways. And that, grudgingly, these same individuals had later agreed that perhaps the destruction of the binding had been a *good* thing.

"I like--" Malachi struggled for words. "I like to play with Eri." He hesitated. "I would read to her, but I can't. So I make up stories."

"What kind of stories?" Now he piqued my interest. A librarian's first love is stories, after all, closely followed by research.

"I tell her what I know of Faerie," Malachi said, relaxing now that I hadn't mocked his devotion to his charge. "And I make up adventures." A small smile touched his lips. "Eri the Bold." The smile broadened. "I think she likes my stories."

"I imagine she would," I said. "Eri's a lucky little girl." Not only did she have loving parents, she had the rest of the Hunt as well to dote on her every desire. Some children didn't even have the loving parents part of the equation, especially in this modern day and age.

An idea slowly formed in my mind. "We have an after-school program here at the library. It's sponsored by a local non-profit daycare, and we provide programming for the children twice a week."

Malachi cocked his head. "And a daycare is--?"

"This particular one is for low-income families," I said. "Families who might not be able to afford childcare, even if both parents have jobs." My mind recalled his question. "A daycare is a place where children can stay while their parents are at work. Most of them are prohibitively expensive."

"I think I understand," Malachi said. "But humans' ability to leave their children with strangers--how do they feel when something happens to their child?"

"Guilty, I'm sure," I said. Having no children of my own, it was a bit difficult for me to relate. "But there aren't as many stay-at-home mothers today, or fathers, for that matter. Most of them *have* to work, or else there would be no food on the table." I truly had no desire to participate in an argument concerning the pros and cons of childcare with a member of the Wild Hunt.

"You mentioned a program your library provides," Malachi said. "What do you do?"

"We--well, the youth librarians tell them stories. Sometimes we have guests come in, local authors or artists. Or storytellers." Which was why I'd had the idea in the first place. Most of the local authors and artists in town had day jobs to make ends meet. It was difficult at times to schedule a guest even once a month.

"And you want me to do what?" Malachi asked. "Tell them stories?"

"To prove that you're not a bad person?" I countered. "But of course."

He opened his mouth, I thought, to refuse. And then something passed across his face, an emotion I could not interpret. He bit his lip and looked down at his clenched hands.

"How many children?"

"Between ten and fifteen, most days," I said. "We run the program on Tuesdays and Thursdays."

I watched him do a quick calculation in his head. "Tomorrow is Thursday."

"Yes."

"What time?"

"Four o'clock. The program usually runs until five." Would he accept? The Hunt was mercurial in its strangeness. What seemed normal for them one day changed the next. I could no more predict how Malachi would reply than I could predict which book would become the next bestseller.

Malachi took a deep breath. "I will come."

And he did come. He was waiting for me when I pulled into my parking spot the next morning.

I climbed out of my car. I'd even beat Penny to work, which should have been engraved on a plaque and bolted to the front door for everyone to see.

"Good morning, Malachi."

He wore different clothing today, greens and browns that would blend into the backdrop of the forest. He carried a long polished stick, too, the Hunt's version of a blind man's cane.

"Ms. Montgomery." He nodded in my direction. "I thought I would come to familiarize myself with the library before this afternoon--if I have your permission, of course."

I would have to warn the librarians on duty, just so they wouldn't think it strange for a member of the Wild Hunt to be roaming the halls.

"This is a public building, Malachi. We can't keep you out, even if you have library fines." My poor attempt at a joke flew right over his head. "Are you staying all day?"

"If I may," he said. "I requested, and received, permission to come." He indicated a small tote bag at his feet. "Emle asked that I return our library books."

"Well, then I'll give you a tour," I said. "We don't *officially* open for another hour, but I doubt the Director will mind."

Malachi stiffened. "She's already here?"

"No. She's on vacation." Receiving one hundred and nine pounds of gold from the elves as payment for a bargain made almost two centuries ago had certainly made things interesting around the library. After most of the interest had died down, Ivy had created an exhibit using one of the gold coins. The director had taken to standing in front of the display for hours on end, muttering about gold. "So I'm in charge for the time being."

"Dragons don't care for Hounds," Malachi explained as he picked up the tote bag. "Although I've never been able to figure out why. We never Hunted *them*."

I would not pretend to know the reasons behind the dragons' displeasure. So far, the only dragon I'd met was the Director, and I half-hoped it would stay that way. If our Director was any indication, dragons were eccentric, inhuman even in human form, and had a fetish for gold that no amount of money could satisfy.

"You've been here before, so interrupt me if I tell you something you already know," I said. "Let's go in the front door. That would make it easier to show you around."

We walked around the building to the front door. Malachi seemed to have no trouble navigating the steps or the sidewalk. But he *had* been to the library before. And perhaps I should stop marvelling that he knew his way around. It probably didn't hurt that he was a member of the Wild Hunt who could shift shape on a whim. After all, blind *humans* got around just fine on *their* own.

I gave him the complete tour, both the public and private sections of the library, and left him listening to an audiobook in the media room with instructions to ask for me if he needed any help. Then I retired to my office to collect my messages and pretend I was a *normal* Assistant Director in a *normal* small Ohio library system.

I am 80% certain I forgot to eat lunch.

At three forty-five, Penny buzzed my office to tell me that Malachi was waiting in the reception area. I hurried out to meet him.

"I'm sorry, Malachi. I should have asked if you brought any lunch. I've been--busy." It was a poor excuse for ignoring him all day.

"I'm fine," he said, tense again. "Are you certain this is a good idea?"

"Did the Hunt eat children?" I asked, only half-kidding. And forgetting to keep my voice down, by Penny's shocked gasp.

"Of course not!" Now I'd offended him, but he seemed to regain some of his courage.

"Then let's go," I said. "Do you remember the way?"

As soon as we walked through the door to the meeting room, I realized something had changed. Mrs. Green, the elderly lady who usually brought the children to the library, was gone. In her place was a young woman wearing a gauzy silk dress straight out of a Maxfield Parrish painting. Her honey-blond hair fell down her back in thick waves, and she wore dainty slippers on her feet. She did not look the type to be an employee at a daycare. Any child *she* would have would be raised by a nanny and have carefully organized play dates with his or her peers.

She smiled at me as I entered. "Good afternoon. You must be Ms. Montgomery. I've heard a lot about you from my aunt."

"Your aunt?" My mind did not want to connect old Mrs. Green with this beautiful young lady. I wondered what Malachi would think, forgetting for a moment that he was blind.

"Mrs. Green. I'm Jenny." She held out her hand. Golden bracelets gently clinked together on both wrists.

"Pleased to meet you," I said, and shook. Her grip was soft, but firm. And from the way the children quietly awaited the start of Malachi's storytelling, I revised my opinion of her child-caring skills.

Her smile slipped a little when Malachi stepped into the room. For a moment, I thought she would say something--denounce him as a Hound, perhaps, but she pasted her smile back on and clasped her hands together.

"My aunt is training me to take over her business," she whispered.

She certainly didn't sound very happy about it. And behind me, I heard a low growl slip through Malachi's lips.

I turned. Malachi stood in the doorway, his white-knuckled grip on his stick his only sign of distress.

"I didn't know there was anything special planned for the children today," Jenny continued, her voice just as unhappy as before. "Aunt Janet said this would be a good day for me to come."

"And do what with them?" Malachi asked. Even his voice held an echo of a growl.

Jenny's face crumpled. "We just got back from the park."

I saw the children watching this mind-boggling scene with a growing sense of unease. One of the little girls bit her lip. In a moment, they would all start to cry, and then I would have to figure out a way to make them stop. I liked children--don't get me wrong--but I was an only child and had none of my own.

"Malachi's quite a good storyteller," I said, trying to steer the conversation back on solid ground. "I'm sorry we couldn't tell you about this in advance, but it was all a bit last-minute."

"I love children," Jenny whispered.

"I'm sure you do." Malachi sounded so much like his Master that I had to look twice to make sure Gabriel had not appeared.

"You don't understand!" Jenny's voice did not rise above a whisper. "You don't know how hard it is to survive!"

It took me a bit to catch on. "Wait a second. Are you--"

A small hand tugged on my skirt. I glanced down to find a little girl staring up at me, her big brown eyes wide.

"Jenny's a fairy princess," she said, loud enough for the other children to hear.

I glanced at Jenny. "A fairy princess?"

She flushed. "Well. Not exactly." She took the little girl's hand despite Malachi's warning growl. "Go sit down, Rianna. Everything--" her voice shook, just a little. "Everything will be just fine."

"Do I need to call one of the youth librarians in to tell them a story while you two work things out?" I asked. The name 'Jenny Green' didn't ring any bells, nor did her style of dress. If she was a supernatural being, I didn't know which mythology she'd fit into. I had been doing some research on my days off, but even this library's collection was not complete.

Malachi folded his arms. "We've killed your kind before."

Jenny raised her chin. "I know you have. But we've changed."

They were both ignoring me. I sighed, pushed past Malachi, and motioned to one of the librarians. Once she was safely entrenched with a pile of books and a few of our new handpuppets, I stepped in between Malachi and Jenny. "You two are coming with me."

As soon as I had them alone in the small meeting room, Malachi's lips drew back in a snarl. "Did you think you could hide from the Council like this? How transparent can you *be*?"

Jenny opened her mouth to reply, but I cut her off.

"Wait a second." Now I could define myself as a referee as well as a psychiatrist. Psychologist. Whatever. "This is *my* library, and *I'm* the one in charge. Explain."

Malachi hesitated.

"Now," I ordered, trying my best to sound like his Master.

"Jenny Greenteeth," Malachi snapped. "A Water Hag. Notorious for one thing: stealing and eating children." He bared his teeth. "Look her up in your books, if you wish. And then you'll see."

I glanced at Jenny, whose face had frozen at his condemnation. "Is this true?"

Jenny licked her lips. "M-my aunt has been in business for almost ten years. And she's not lost a single child."

"Outside Council control," Malachi said. "They don't even know you're here, do they?"

Jenny shook her head. "Aunt Janet said it was too risky. That they'd drive us out. Or kill us. If we were to survive, we'd have to change. And so we have."

"You expect me to believe that?" Malachi asked. "My Master killed one of your kind less than a year ago at the lake. And I heard her *speak* of sweet little lost children and what she had done to them."

"Not one of *my* kind," Jenny whispered. "There are other Water Hags, and plenty of creatures who eat children." Her eyes flashed. "And what would those same books say about the Hunt?"

Malachi opened his mouth to reply, then closed it again. He cocked his head. "You are truly--caring for these children?"

"I would guard them with my life while they are in my care," Jenny said. "Tell the Council if you wish. They will cast us out, or kill us, and these children will return to empty homes after school. And perhaps fall prey to humans that are worse monsters than we will *ever* be." When Malachi did not reply, her voice softened. "It is our atonement, this small thing we do for them. For the children who *did* get eaten."

"Let me get this straight," I said. "You're a--" What had Malachi called her? "A Water Hag? And you used to eat children?"

Jenny nodded. "That's right."

"And now you--is your aunt a Water Hag, too? Nice little old Mrs. Green?"

"'Nice little old Mrs. Green' probably ate a dozen children a month," Malachi said stiffly.

Jenny glared at him. "And how many people did *you* kill?" She put her hands on her hips. "You're all the same. Ready to convict us without cause. If I didn't know any better, I'd say you *were* a member of the Council. You're certainly *acting* like one."

Malachi growled at her. "You dare--"

"Wait just one minute!" I had no desire to be torn limb from limb by an angry Hound and a furious Water Hag, but their bickering was getting on my nerves. "Jenny has a point. A very *good* point. Malachi, you came here because you said the Hunt has changed. Why is it such a stretch to believe Water Hags can change as well?"

"She could be lying," Malachi said. "I've heard they're good at that."

"Just as your Master could be lying to you," I said. "Just as *you* could be lying to me."

Malachi's face paled. "No. I would never--"

I touched his arm. "But you could have."

He jerked away from me and stumbled against a table that someone had slid against one wall. His stick clattered to the floor. I picked it up, not knowing how I should try to reassure him.

Not knowing if I could. Some battles were better fought alone, after all.

"You could truthspell me and find my words are true," Jenny said. "Is it so bad that others have learned from your example?"

Malachi stiffened. "Our example. If the Council had not bound us--" he hesitated. "If the Council had not bound us, we would still terrorize these forests."

"Or you'd be dead. You don't really know what would have happened, because it didn't happen," I said. "If it makes you feel any better, I've met Mrs. Green many times and I've never seen her mistreat a child. In fact, I've never seen her raise her voice to a child. They all seem to like her, and they obey her. Not out of fear. Out of love. And respect."

"I should never have come here," Malachi whispered, bowing his head. "I should never have come." He leaned against the table, his arms bearing most of his weight. "I'm sorry. You're right. I've treated you no better than I expect to be treated by others. Who am I to say whether or not you're telling the truth? I am just a Hound, nothing more."

"And both of us are attempting to make our way in this world without falling into darkness," Jenny said. "I bear you no ill will."

Malachi nodded without speaking. When he bent to fumble for his stick, I handed it back to him.

"Are you still willing to tell the children a story?" I asked.

"Any story I tell them now would be a sad story," Malachi said. "I think it's time for me to leave." He slipped out the door before I could stop him. By the time I regained my wits enough to follow him, he was gone.

Jenny's charges were picked up by their parents by five-thirty. Not a single parent questioned her capabilities or species. And all the children seemed well-adjusted and happy to believe that their caregiver was a fairy princess, a creature of the light instead of the dark.

For three days, nothing unusual happened in the library system. A clerk left on maternity leave, Ivy delivered a building inspection report on all four branches, and I spent my waking hours poring over facts and figures and trying to come up with a proposal to bring before the board concerning two new buildings. Since it was my first proposal of this kind--the Director had given the entire responsibility to me--I wanted it to be perfect, of course.

Bright and early Monday morning, I pulled into the parking lot--before Penny for the second time in my life--and saw Malachi waiting for me.

I climbed out of my car. "Malachi? I didn't think I'd see you back."

"Did you see the news this weekend?"

I'd spent the entire weekend holed up in my apartment with the TV off. The newspapers still lay on my dining room table, unread.

"No, I didn't. What happened?" Whatever had happened could not have concerned the Hunt--the Council would never allow a newspaper article or newscast to spill that particular pot of beans.

"A little girl vanished yesterday afternoon," Malachi said. "She was last seen playing with her dog in her backyard." He waited for that to sink in before delivering his coup de gras. "Her name is Rianna Morgan."

My mind flashed to wide brown eyes and pigtails. "*That* Rianna?"

"The very same." His voice was thick with some unexpressed emotion I dared not name.

"You don't think--" I didn't want to finish the sentence.

His face closed completely. "I hope not."

But what if we'd both been wrong? What if Jenny Green, a.k.a. Jenny Greenteeth *had* lied to us? Maybe I should have realized, or known not to trust her. I *had* researched. I knew the living myths and legends could be tricky. And I knew the Council's treaties between species were just signatures on a piece of paper, easily broken.

If she *had* lied to us, and if we'd both blithely gone on our way without another thought, I would never be able to forgive myself.

I saw an inkling of what Malachi had to live with, just in that one thought.

"The Hunt is searching for her," Malachi said. "I'm supposed to be at home. Useless. I can't help but think this is too much of a coincidence, but I have to know."

"Why is the *Hunt* searching for her?" I asked. "What about the police?"

Malachi's grin was truly terrible. "Would you trust *humans* to search this forest knowing what you know about those who live within it?"

"Well, no," I said. "But I don't understand why it has to be *you*. You don't know she was taken by anything--or anyone--supernatural. She could have just wandered off."

"The owner of the daycare she attends is a Water Hag," Malachi said. "And anyway, the forest falls under our jurisdiction. We've found other lost children in the months we've been free."

I wondered how many missing children had supernatural connections. Knowing what I knew, which seemed to be very little at times, I would safely bet two out of three.

"Do you know where Jenny Green lives?" So much for beating Penny to work. A lost little girl was much more important than which of us could get up earlier. And I'd never told Penny that we were competing in a contest, anyway. It was much more fun to have a silent victory than to suffer through smug assuredness, since she won nine and a half times out of ten.

"I--took the liberty of finding out," Malachi admitted. "I did not intend to use my knowledge. But now--now I have to."

"I'm going with you, then," I said, opening my car door. "I'll drive. You can navigate."

Malachi hesitated. "If she lied to us--"

"If she lied to us, she'll have the Council to answer to," I said, sick at heart. "Come on."

Greenlake Nursery was not a landscaping business; that much was obvious. Acre-long, manmade lakes surrounded both sides of the gravel driveway. Beyond the lakes, deep forest stretched as far as I could see.

At the end of the driveway sat a small cottage made of local stone. Children's toys--two swing-sets, a log cabin playhouse, a half dozen baby pools, plastic balls, and toy cars--littered the front and side yards.

At this hour of the morning, we were the only visitors in evidence.

Something niggled at the back of my mind, but I didn't realize what was odd about the scene until I exited my car. "There's no electricity back here?"

"Magic is cheaper than electricity," Malachi said, unconcerned. *"We* don't have electricity either." He scented the air, a strange sight for a Hound in human form. "But I smell--something. Someone here is cooking."

In fact, if I squinted, I could barely see a wisp of smoke rising above the trees. Coming from the backyard. Cooking. Did Water Hags cook?

When no one challenged us, I followed Malachi around the side of the house, moving around a veritable obstacle course of toys. The backyard was surprisingly clean and neat, with a rambling herb garden and a stone path leading into the forest. And a huge, freestanding beehive oven made out of the same stone.

That wisp of smoke came from the oven. And it was in use--even *I* could feel the heat from where we stood.

"This isn't good," Malachi whispered. "I sense--heat. Tell me what you see."

I described the oven to the best of my abilities. *Huge* and *hot* came to mind. So did the fact that the door to the oven was big enough to fit a full-grown man.

Malachi grimaced. "We're going to have to open it."

"No need." Jenny's voice came from behind us. "Aunt Janet's already gone."

I turned around. Jenny Green stood on the bank of one of the lakes, dripping wet but wearing a dress similar to the one she had worn at the library. Her hair hung in dark tangles today, though, and her eyes were rimmed with red.

From weeping? Where had her aunt gone?

"What do you mean?" Malachi asked.

Jenny wiped her eyes. "There's only one way for a Water Hag to die," she whispered. "Aunt Janet was alive for four hundred and eleven years. She said four hundred and eleven years was long enough."

I glanced from Jenny to the oven and back again. My mind kept getting stuck on *Hansel and Gretel.* Nice old Mrs. Green? Who just happened to be a Water Hag? Gone?

"Water Hags need water to survive," Malachi said softly. "So it makes sense that burning would be the only way to die."

"That's--terrible!" I said. "I *liked* your aunt! She was a lovely old lady!" Who had once eaten children. But still.

"It's difficult to survive in this world sometimes," Malachi whispered, his face turned towards the oven.

Had he thought about ending *his* life? Would he have committed suicide if Gabriel had cast him out?

For a moment, I thought he wouldn't ask about Rianna. "Did your aunt take a snack in the oven with her?"

"A--" Jenny's face paled. "A *what?*"

"Rianna Morgan is missing," I said, feeling horrible for even asking. "Since she came here for daycare--"

"We wondered if you knew anything about her disappearance," Malachi said. Through some miracle, he kept his voice calm and even. Not a single thread of anger escaped.

Jenny opened her mouth, closed it, then opened it again. Two spots of color bloomed high on her cheeks. She clenched her fists. "I can't *believe* you're asking me that question!"

"The Council would ask a lot more," Malachi said. "And I *know* you don't want to get them involved. Are there children coming today?"

"No. Not today. Not for a week, in fact. Aunt Janet already made arrangements for their care." She flushed. "And they weren't the arrangements you're thinking about!"

I hadn't been thinking about any arrangements, but a whole host of horrible images obligingly appeared in reply to her protest.

"Where is Rianna Morgan, Jenny?" A growl now lurked behind his words. "The Council is much worse than the Hunt will ever be."

"Then you're going to have to tell them about me," Jenny snapped. "Because I haven't seen Rianna Morgan since Friday afternoon when her father picked her up. Aunt Janet was already busy loading wood in the oven by then. When did she disappear?"

"Late yesterday afternoon," Malachi said.

Jenny folded her arms. "There. That clears me, then. Aunt Janet went into the oven Saturday morning. And I've been here watching over the fire since then." She sniffed. "To be charitable, let me check Aunt Janet's files and see if anything sticks out about Rianna Morgan. She's such a sweet little girl."

For some reason, hearing her say that struck me as wrong. Like someone choosing a sweet little lobster to eat. Or a sweet little kitten, for that matter. But I didn't say anything. I was willing to give anyone the benefit of my doubt, especially after what had happened last time.

Jenny walked across the grass to the side door, leaving a trail of water behind. "After that question you asked, I truly don't feel like inviting you inside, but I don't want you poking around out here either. Come in." She glanced back at us with a predatory smile. "I promise not to eat you."

The interior of a Water Hag's human-style home was not very different from anyone else's home, save for the abundance of aquariums that seemed to have space on every wall. A wholly modern fridge sat in the kitchen next to a gas oven and a small microwave. The kitchen table was cluttered with unopened mail and a cream colored envelope bearing Jenny's name. Clumps of herbs hung to dry over the sink. And a small cobalt blue bottle sat on the windowsill, a single dandelion proudly erect in its narrow mouth.

Childish drawings layered a bulletin board above the kitchen table. A few of the drawings were signed, but I didn't see one marked *Rianna*.

"Wait here," Jenny said. "I'll be right back."

Malachi felt for a chair and sat down. "What do you see? I smell nothing amiss here."

"It's a kitchen," I said. "A normal kitchen. With a stove, a fridge, and a microwave. There's mail on the table about three inches from your left elbow. There's a bulletin board above you with drawings from the children on it." I studied the lot. "Most of them seem to depict this house and the lakes. A couple are more--inventive."

"Inventive in what way?" Malachi asked.

"Well, one seems to depict some sort of fire-breathing monster. Another one has stick figures with long hair floating above the lake." I flipped the top ones aside. "Here's one that looks like a rendition of Rapunzel's tower, complete with hair. And this one here--" Four layers down, a carefully drawn family. A father, marked *Daddy* in a childish script. A little girl, marked *Me*. And a large tree with arms, marked *Mommy*.

The drawing was signed *Rianna*.

"What is it?"

I carefully unpinned the drawing and described it to him. "I don't know anything about Rianna or her parents, but don't you think it's a bit odd for her to draw her mother as a tree?"

"Not as odd as you might think," Jenny said from the doorway. She stepped into the kitchen, holding a manila folder in one hand. "Aunt Janet's nothing but thorough in documenting her charges. And according to her notes, Rianna's mother abandoned her a week after she was born."

"But a *tree?*" I asked.

"Rianna talks to trees," Jenny said. "And flowers. And plants."

"A lot of little children talk to trees," Malachi said. "That means nothing." He stood and pushed his chair away. "We're wasting time."

"Do the trees talk back to these other children?" Jenny asked. She brandished the file folder in Malachi's face. "Because they talk back to Rianna."

Malachi sat back down. "Well, then."

"But what does that mean?" I asked, still clutching Rianna's drawing in one hand. "What does that have to do with this picture?"

"Maybe nothing," Malachi said. "But it might be a good idea to check with someone--the Council, perhaps--and see if there have been any reports of dryads in the forest."

"Dryads?" For once I knew that name. "Tree spirits?"

"Must you involve the Council?" Jenny asked. "We *could* ask Rianna's father--"

"He might not have known," Malachi said. "Or if he did know, he might not tell us. The Hunt isn't--trusted. Even now."

"Perhaps if you tried to be more friendly more people would trust you," Jenny said.

I couldn't find a shred of sarcasm in her voice.

Malachi sighed. "I'm afraid it's a bit too late for that." He tried to smile. "After a thousand years of pain and suffering, it's difficult to convince anyone that you've changed."

"I feel the same way," Jenny said quietly.

For a moment, they were both on the same page of the same book. I sensed a shared connection between them now, the same obstacles to overcome; the same dark past to remember.

I glanced at my watch. "I'm due in at work in forty-five minutes. Jenny, do you have a phone?"

"Of course," she said, leaving me to wonder how magic could conjure phone lines as well as electricity.

"Can I borrow it? I'll call in sick or take a personal day. The library can run without me for twenty-four hours."

"But I thought you said you were in charge," Malachi said, confused.

"I did." I dialed the number as I spoke. "But I'm not leaving you to go to the Council by yourself, especially if we're leaving Jenny out of it."

He exhaled. "Good. Thank you."

After I'd reassured Penny that I would definitely be in tomorrow, was not dying, and had not spent the weekend in the hospital, I hung up the phone and carefully folded Rianna's drawing.

"Let's go, Malachi."

He stood. "If the Council gives us a good lead, we'll come back for you," he promised Jenny.

"And you'll leave me out of this?" She didn't quite wring her hands, but I could tell she was worried.

"We'll leave you out of this," I said. It was as close to a promise as I could come.

Ivy had described the Council like this: Because of the fact that they had bound the Wild Hunt and tamed them, each and every supernatural person who lived in or near Beth-Hill did not dare to cross the Council for fear they would make their lives miserable.

From the elves, I'd discovered that while this much was true, there were only four Council members now--one of those inactive--and that a century ago, the binding of the Hunt had killed five of their number. The Hunt had lost ten Hounds to that binding. It was unlikely the Council would ever be able to pull off such a feat ever again.

But no one challenged them, for the Council kept the peace between the super and natural worlds. And thus they were useful, up to a point.

Lucas Lane, the only Council member I'd ever spoken to, lived in a small stone cottage on the edge of the state park that surrounded Beth-Hill. He was an elderly man, nice enough, I suppose, but just as inscrutable as the Hunt when it came to giving straight answers to certain questions. But as the Council Historian, if anyone would know about dryads in the forest, it would be Lucas.

Malachi kept silent until I stopped the car in front of Lucas' house.

"My brothers are still looking for her," he said. "So far, they've found no sign of a trail."

"Would that be surprising if she talks to trees and they answer?" I asked. "Couldn't she have asked them to cover her trail?" I still wanted to believe that she'd wandered into the forest on her own, not that some unknown non-reformed monster had taken her.

"It's possible," Malachi allowed. "But this is a child, Ms. Montgomery. She's only four." He gripped his stick, his knuckles white.

Somehow, she'd seemed a lot older than four at the library, with her talk about fairy princesses.

"I doubt Lucas will mind us asking," I said. "Are you ready?"

"I am never *ready* to face the Council," Malachi whispered. "But if we have a chance to find Rianna--then I am ready." He opened the passenger side door.

By the time I closed my door, Lucas was waiting for us on the porch, his face alight with curiosity.

"To what do I owe the pleasure of your company?"

For a moment I couldn't tell if he was being sarcastic or if he was genuinely pleased to see us.

Malachi stiffened, just a little. "If you have seen the news reports, you know why we have come."

"Ah. The little girl." Lucas nodded. "I heard the Hunt last night, and I wondered if you had found her yet."

To his credit, he didn't ask why Malachi was not with the others, searching the forest for any sign of Rianna.

"She's still missing, but Malachi and I found a clue," I said. "We were hoping you might be able to shed some light on our discovery."

"Indeed." Lucas stepped away from the porch railing. "Why don't you both come in and make yourselves comfortable?"

I started towards the porch stairs, but Malachi didn't move.

"Malachi?"

"No." His voice cracked. "Oh, no." He turned away, dropped his stick, and fell to his knees.

"Malachi, what did they find?" Lucas' voice snapped my paralysis. I glanced at him, then went to Malachi.

"What's wrong? What happened?"

His shoulders shook. "They--Nathaniel found--Rianna's dead. I have to go."

Before I could stop him, he shifted into a Hound and ran off into the forest.

I stared after him, my mouth agape. I hadn't really *seen* one of the Hounds shift yet, and he had just shifted right in front of my face.

"Did you see--" I remembered Lucas was a member of the Council and smiled, a bit embarrassed. "I'm sorry. I'm sure you've seen that before." Malachi's words hit home, leaving me with a hollow emptiness in my stomach. "Damn it. He said Nathaniel found her, and she was dead."

"I heard," Lucas said quietly. "If you'd like to come in, we can wait for the Hunt to arrive."

"To arrive?" I asked, glancing back at the forest where Malachi had vanished. How did he navigate as a Hound? Through smell alone?

"They'll bring the body here," Lucas said. "I'll have to find out how she died, and then I will concoct a story that will satisfy the authorities."

"You do that? Make up stories that the public will believe?" I stared at him.

Lucas smiled, albeit sadly. "How do you think they came up with the swamp gas theory to explain away UFOs?"

Before I could splutter an undignified reply to that question, he turned and walked back into the house.

I had no true choice but to follow.

Thirty minutes later, Nathaniel appeared out of the forest, carrying a small bundle in his arms. He did not seem surprised when I met him at the door.

"Lucas said you can lay her on the couch," I whispered, fighting back tears at the sight of those smooth brown pigtails. She wore jeans and a pink t-shirt that was spotted with mud. Her feet were bare, but Nathaniel produced a tiny pair of flip-flops from one pocket after he arranged her body on the couch.

Her mouth was half-open, showing baby teeth that would never have a chance to fall out, and her eyes, thank goodness, were closed.

"Where did you find her?" Lucas asked, appearing out of the kitchen as I tried to blink my tears away.

"Near the center of the forest," Nathaniel replied. "At the foot of a cliff. I think--she must have slipped and fallen. Her neck is broken."

"Not murdered, then? A simple accident?" Lucas sighed. "Thank goodness. I've called Michael and Niklas already. They should be here within the hour."

I sank down in a chair. Something crackled in my pocket, and I pulled out Rianna's folded drawing. The clue we'd never had a chance to decipher.

"What's that?" Nathaniel asked when I unfolded it.

"Malachi and I found this," I said, then realized Malachi might not have told anyone that he had disobeyed Gabriel's orders to stay behind. I waited for the outcry, but Nathaniel only nodded.

"He told me he was with you," he said.

"It's a picture Rianna's drew of her family," I said. "Only, we thought it was strange, because she drew her mother as a tree." I couldn't raise my head and risk seeing her body. It was heartbreaking enough to realize she would never pick up a crayon again.

"A tree? Let me see that." Lucas held out his hand.

I gave him the drawing and stared at the floor. Then out the window. Anywhere but at the body on the couch. "According to--our source, Rianna's mother abandoned her at birth. And Rianna talked to trees."

"Your source?" Lucas asked, but didn't press me for a name. "A lot of children talk to trees."

"Our source said the trees don't usually answer back." I shrugged. "We intended to ask you about tree spirits living in the forest, but that doesn't really matter now. She's dead."

"Hmmm." Lucas lay the drawing on the coffee table. "Nathaniel, where is Malachi?"

"Back at the house," Nathaniel said a moment later. "In the garden, sitting by the fishpond."

"Will you ask him to come here, please?" Lucas tapped Rianna's drawing with one finger. "I have a question that I'm afraid only Malachi can adequately answer. But I have one for you as well, Nathaniel."

"He will come," Nathaniel said after another silent communication. "What is your question?"

I envied the Hounds their bond. It would be so much easier to contact your friends and family by telepathy instead of mundane means. And it would cut down on the phone bills for everyone involved.

"When you found her, did you find her as a human or a Hound?"

"I found one shoe at the top of the cliff as a Hound," Nathaniel said. "I shifted, and saw her below as a human."

I didn't see the point of Lucas' question. "What does that have to do with anything? It's very obvious she's dead."

Lucas smiled. "Just wait until Malachi gets here, and then you'll see. If I'm correct, this isn't over. If I'm not, then we'll all sit down and figure out a story that will satisfy her father and everyone else."

Malachi arrived fifteen minutes later, loping up to the porch in Hound form and shifting into human form to tackle the stairs. I saw him hesitate before he knocked on the screen door.

"Lucas? Nathaniel said you wanted to ask me a question?"

"I am in need of your nose, Malachi," Lucas said, opening the door to let him in. "Nathaniel brought back Rianna's body. Can you tell me where it is?"

Malachi's forehead furrowed. "Is this some sort of a trick?"

I glanced at Nathaniel, who looked just as confused.

"No trick, I swear to you," Lucas said. "Just tell me where the body lies."

Still suspicious, Malachi scented the air. I expected him to walk right over to the couch, but he stood in the doorway and frowned at Lucas. "I don't smell anything."

"Try it as a Hound, just to make sure," Lucas suggested.

Obligingly, Malachi shifted. Even though I was ready for it this time, I still jumped.

A moment later, he shifted again. "There's no body in this room."

"Come with me," Lucas said, and took Malachi's hand. He led the Hound over to the couch, and slowly lowered Malachi's hand until it touched Rianna's still form.

Malachi jumped back and almost collided with the coffee table. "What kind of a trick is this?"

"No trick," Lucas said grimly. "Or, rather, no trick of mine. What you felt--what the rest of us see--is not Rianna Morgan's body."

"Then what is it?" I asked. Because it sure would have fooled me.

"Years ago, it would have been called a changeling," Lucas said. "They're rare now, and quite illegal."

"So someone created this--duplicate of Rianna's body and put it at the foot of the cliff so everyone would think she had fallen and died?" I asked, risking a glance at the body. It still *looked* like Rianna to me. But I was no expert in identifying corpses. Thank goodness that particular job had never come up in my line of work.

"Exactly," Lucas said. "Two questions remain, however: who and why?" He picked up Rianna's drawing. "This picture you found just might contain a clue after all. But Malachi--"

Malachi's head rose. "Yes?"

"Ms. Montgomery spoke of a source who gave you this drawing?" His voice was deceptively mild. "I will need to speak with this source of yours. As soon as possible."

"I swore we'd leave her out of this," Malachi said, standing his ground. "And I'm not going back on my word."

"Our source really has nothing to do with this," I said in his defence. "And I'm not going to betray her trust either."

"You both do realize that I'm being very *courteous* in asking for this information nicely," Lucas said, his voice still mild. "I *could* insist, in the interest of saving a child's life."

"I gave my word," Malachi said coldly. "I would not tell you even if my Master ordered me to speak."

Nathaniel gasped. "Malachi!"

"Would you tell your Master, then, so I can be assured that your source truly has nothing to do with this?" Lucas asked.

Malachi hesitated. "No," he finally whispered. "Although I daresay he could tear it from my mind if he wished."

Nathaniel bristled with repressed anger. I half-expected the two Hounds to start a fight, right then and there.

"No, Nathaniel," Malachi said, his voice firming. "I *gave my word*. Surely you--of all people--understand that."

"Look, does *my* word count for anything?" I asked, reminding them all that they were not alone. "I mean, there's a *body* lying on your couch, Lucas. You're telling *me* that it's not really a body, but a changeling, and I'm taking *your* word for it because I wouldn't know the difference between a corpse and a changeling if my life depended on it."

"Your life *may* depend on it, if this source of yours was involved in this deception," Lucas said.

"Nathaniel, stop it!" Malachi growled even though Nathaniel had not said a word. "You may be second-in-command, but you're no stronger than I am. And I will *not* change my mind in this."

Nathaniel folded his arms and scowled at both of us. I tried my best to ignore him.

"We're wasting time," I said. "We could be out looking for Rianna."

Lucas looked like he wanted to take the argument a bit further, but then he saw the look on Malachi's face and subsided.

"I apologize for trying to force you to reveal your source," he said. "But you understand--I'm acting in the child's best interest."

"I know you are," Malachi said, bowing his head. "And so am I. Our source has nothing to do with this."

I tried to force the conversation back on track. "Lucas, what do you know about tree spirits? Dryads?"

Lucas sighed. "There is a grove of oak trees deep in the heart of this forest. Miles, still, from where you found the changeling, Nathaniel."

"Miles? But..." Nathaniel shook his head. "There may be thousands of *acres* in the forest, but--"

"The forest and Faerie are melded together more and more as you travel deeper and deeper into the wilderness," Lucas said. "And it *is* wilderness. I doubt the Hunt has ever traveled that far." He paused to let that sink in. "And traveling so far on the basis of one child's drawing--"

"We cannot leave any stone unturned," Malachi said, his head still bowed. "If there is a chance, however slim, that she is in that oak grove, then we *have* to go."

"Wilderness?" My heart sank as I remembered the last patch of wilderness I'd traveled--in the dark, with a vampire as my companion and a Hound as my guide. And then later on, through Faerie. And that wasn't even considered real wilderness.

"You don't have to go," Malachi said quickly.

Which was true, but could I *not?* How could I return to work without ever knowing what might have happened if I had gone?

Lucas gave me an inscrutable look.

I smiled at him to hide my surge of fear. *At least he hadn't come right out and forbidden me to go.* "I have a suggestion."

"I'm open to suggestions," Lucas said.

"Is there any way you could...discretely ask Rianna's father about her mother before we leave?" I did *not* want to get all the way to this distant oak grove only to discover that Rianna's mother was *not* a dryad.

"I could do that," Lucas said. "And, in fact, I'll do that right now. You were right, Karen. We are wasting time."

Finally, I'd gotten *someone* to call me Karen. "Thank you."

As soon as Lucas vanished into the kitchen, Malachi turned, careful not to stumble and fall on top of the changeling. "You really don't have to go," he said.

"I know. But I'm coming anyway." If I kept my sentences short, perhaps my voice would not shake.

Malachi turned towards Nathaniel. "And you're not coming either."

"What?" Nathaniel stared at him. "Of course I'm coming! You can't--" He bit back the rest of his words.

Which was a smart thing to do, if he was about to say what I *thought* he was about to say.

"You know as well as I do that we will not be welcomed," Malachi said. "If anything, I will be seen as harmless. There *are* advantages to being blind."

Even blind, I wouldn't dare say that Malachi was harmless.

"So you'll wander off into the wilderness with a human as your only companion?" Nathaniel shook his head. "Our Master will refuse to allow you to go."

"No he won't," Malachi said. "And Karen will not be my only companion."

"Who else is going, then?" Nathaniel cried.

"If our source will come, I will welcome her presence," Malachi said.

I felt a little better, knowing that he intended to ask Jenny to accompany us. Surely no one would dare attack a party consisting of a Hound, a Water Hag, and a human. Although, I had a feeling I was the weak link in this particular group.

"Who is your source that you protect so stringently?"

"Someone the Council would persecute if they discovered her presence," Malachi said. "I have no doubts of this."

Nathaniel's anger deflated. "Oh." He grimaced. "You have a sound reasoning for this, but I still don't like it."

Malachi smiled. "Our Master did not like it either, but he, too, saw my reasoning."

"You've already asked?" Nathaniel grinned, his anger forgotten.

"Of course," Malachi said, pretending to be hurt by his doubt. "I would not leave without our Master's permission."

Part of me doubted that, but I held my tongue. It seemed I was holding my tongue a lot these days.

Lucas appeared in the doorway a moment later. "I called Rianna's father."

"And what did he say?" Malachi asked.

"He said her mother claimed to be a gypsy," Lucas said. "And that he met her in the forest a year before Rianna was born."

"And?" Nathaniel asked.

"And less than a week after Rianna's birth, her mother kissed the baby and walked into the forest, never to return."

"So?" I could play this game, too.

"From his descriptions of her, I'd say she fits the general characteristics of some sort of wood spirit," Lucas said. "I can't say if she was a dryad, of course; not without tearing apart this changeling and looking for pertinent clues. However," and here he held up his hand like a lecturer in supernatural physiology. "However, I'd say this is the best lead we have so far. And I wish you luck in your journey."

I doubted we needed the Council's blessing for this particular journey, but again, I held my tongue.

I did take Rianna's drawing from the coffee table and stowed it in my pocket again. Just in case.

Twenty minutes later, Malachi and I were back in my car and on our way to Jenny's house.

My only consolation was that we would not be traveling through the forest in darkness this time. Or, at least not at first.

"Did you really ask Gabriel for permission to go?" I asked as we pulled into Jenny's driveway. If Gabriel had left him behind while the Hunt searched for Rianna in the beginning, what had made him change his mind?

Malachi stared out the window. If I hadn't known he was blind, I would have thought he was watching the play of the sunlight on the lake.

"Malachi?"

"Of course I asked," he whispered, but I sensed some sort of wretched unhappiness in his tone of voice.

I stopped the car. We sat for a moment, me struggling not to voice my doubt, and Malachi staring out the window again. Lost in thoughts of his own.

"Jenny doesn't know about the changeling." I broke the silence before it grew too heavy to bear.

"I know. We'll have to tell her." Malachi gripped his stick with one hand and put his other hand on the door handle. "Whatever happens, Karen-- thank you for coming."

Before I could reply to that, he opened the door, slid out of the car, and started up the path to Jenny's front door.

"Of course I'll come!" Jenny had remained silent through our telling of the finding of the changeling, and what we'd discovered about Rianna's mother. "Although they will not welcome me either. There's no love lost between wood and water."

Which was an interesting way to put it, since wood needed water to grow. But maybe that was part of the problem.

"And thank you for keeping your word. I will admit I had my doubts."

Malachi nodded, accepting both her thanks and her apology.

"There's one problem," I said. Well, there were *many* problems, but this one stuck out in my mind like a four-inch thorn. "You're both not human. I'm sure you can travel much faster than I can. If I come with you--and I *want* to come with you--I'm going to slow you down."

Jenny glanced at Malachi. "That might not be much of a problem, if you really trust me," she said.

"What do you mean?" Malachi asked. "If I didn't trust you, I would have given you up to the Council."

"Likewise," I said. "How can that not be a problem?"

"Contrary to popular belief, Water Hags can change shape into--certain other animals," Jenny said. "The legends got us confused with Phoukas and Kelpies, which are other types of water spirits who can change shape."

"I know what Phoukas and Kelpies are," I said. "I *have* done research. The legends say they can change into horses and that if you ride one--oh." Now I knew why she said 'if you *really* trust me'.

"They drown their victims," Malachi said. "The legends vary on what piece of their victim floats up to the surface of the water. I've heard both the liver and the entrails. And sometimes, the heart."

He almost sounded like he was enjoying himself in telling me this. As if he expected me to chicken out.

I took a deep breath. "I've never ridden a horse before."

"That won't be a problem," Jenny said. "You won't be able to get off until I stop."

That was reassuring.

"That's why you *really* need to trust me," she said when I didn't reply. "If you don't--and I completely understand why you wouldn't--we'll find another way."

Although there didn't seem to *be* another way. I'm sure, given time, the Council or someone else could have come up with a spell or something, but we didn't have any time to spare.

I swallowed every shred of fear that tried to make me refuse. "I trust you."

If my trust was displaced, I'd be dead anyway. Perhaps I'd come back as a ghost and haunt my very own section of the state park.

Perhaps the library board would name a room after me. They would have to commission an artist to paint a picture of my last moments, screaming helplessly as Jenny-the-horse dove into the depths of the lake with me stuck to her back.

I closed my eyes, shook away the images that thought conveyed, and gathered up the remnants of my courage.

"Let's go." *Why* was it always me saying 'let's go'?

Jenny-the-horse had a definite green tinge to her hide. But her overall color matched her hair, honey gold and quite pretty in the sunlight.

I had to drag over a tree stump to mount. And as soon as my left leg touched her other side--the pertinent parts of horses were not in my normal repartee--Jenny leapt into motion. I held on for dear life, even though she'd reassured me time and time again that I *couldn't* fall off.

Malachi, in Hound form, of course, led the way. Circling around the edge of the lake and into the forest, moving so quickly that the trees blurred around me.

And I could not tell he was blind at all.

I don't remember much of our journey. I closed my eyes after the fourth time Jenny jumped over a yawning chasm at breakneck speed.

Malachi must have been following some sort of trail, because he never faltered in his stride.

When Jenny finally slowed to a trot, I cracked open my eyes and stared in wonder at what the forest had become.

Towering trees--I couldn't name a single one--loomed overhead, wreathed in Spanish moss and grapevines as thick as my wrists.

This was not forest that man had lumbered. This was *virgin* forest, the like of which I'd never seen.

"Oh, my," I whispered. "This is in *Ohio*?"

Malachi shifted and regarded me with no small amount of humor. "Not exactly. I think this place borders Faerie in some parts. In others--in others, I guess it *is* in Ohio."

Faerie hadn't left much of an impression on me. But this place--these trees--they would haunt my dreams forever.

It *almost* made me want to go back to school and get a degree in Forestry or something, just to have the chance to be near them again.

I stared up at the canopy of leaves above us, and realized that the forest was completely silent. No birdcalls echoed through the branches. No squirrels scolded us for disturbing their paradise.

"It's awfully quiet," I whispered.

Jenny stopped. I slid off her back and tried to make my legs remember how to walk. By the time I'd gotten all my limbs sorted out, she'd shifted into human shape.

A sudden wind whipped through the trees, furious enough to pepper us with leaf mold and small branches. I covered my face with my hands and sought shelter against the trunk of a nearby tree.

"They know we're here," Malachi said as soon as the wind died down.

Jenny shook leaves from her hair. "Surely not."

This time, I couldn't miss the sarcasm in her tone of voice.

"Knowing we're here is a bad thing?" I asked. "Could they have missed us? This doesn't look like a place many hikers see."

"It isn't," Malachi said. "You're probably the first human to set foot on this ground." He did not smile. "Pray that you're not the *last* human as well."

I tried to hide my shiver behind the act of brushing more twigs off the back of my shirt. "Where to now?"

"Straight ahead," Malachi said. "Do you see where the sun breaks through the canopy right over there? I can feel its heat from here. And I have a feeling we'll find what we're looking for--or not--over that ridge."

That 'ridge' was a steep hill stretching up into more forest. I did see a flash of blue sky, however, at the top of the hill, barely visible through the thick trees.

"We'll walk, I think," Jenny said. "It's not far, and we should stick together."

I didn't disagree with her. Sticking together--and walking--sounded just fine to me.

So we walked, slipping and sliding on wet leaves and mud. The very ground seemed to rebel against our presence, and most of the trees had grown thorns when I wasn't looking.

Malachi and Jenny weren't having any better luck in the ascent. Evidently, the forest didn't like visitors. Or else the dryads--or whatever they were-- waiting for us at the top of the hill wanted to keep us out.

Not that I blamed them. If I had stolen a little girl and left an illegal changeling in her place, I wouldn't want anyone to find me either.

I sliced my arm on a thorn and split the palm of my right hand open on another. Malachi slipped and fell, sliding five feet down the hill before he stopped his descent with the aid of a sapling. Jenny's gauzy dress was in tatters by the time we pushed through the last stand of trees into sunlight--and into the waiting arms of a dozen archers dressed in greens and browns, their nut-brown faces intent on our capture.

Or our deaths, I suppose. At that moment, though, I was trying to guide my thoughts away from death.

I froze. Jenny froze. Malachi, who couldn't see the archers, took one step forward before I could stop him.

An arrow whistled an inch past his ear. He stopped, scented the air, and stood very, very still.

"There are a dozen archers," I whispered, trying not to move my lips.

"Not elves," Jenny said, also keeping her voice low. "Tree spirits of some kind, I'd guess."

Thank goodness we hadn't broken any branches or uprooted any seedlings on our way up the hill.

We stood there for a long minute, both sides unwilling to make the first move. When neither Malachi nor Jenny took the initiative to speak, I took one very small step forward and raised my hands to show them they were empty.

"We come in peace." Hey, it was a start.

"No, you don't," a new voice said--a female voice. "Humans *never* come here in peace. The Wild Hunt has never known peace, and Water Hags are our mortal enemies and will not find peace within this forest."

I glanced at Jenny when the lady who had spoken did not appear. "Did you know you were their mortal enemy?"

"It has something to do with one of my ancient ancestors," she murmured. "I don't know the details."

"But you came anyway?" Malachi asked. He caught himself before he turned around.

"Rianna was in *my* charge!" Jenny hissed. "And Aunt Janet never lost a single child!"

"Bring them," the voice said, bored now. "Alive, if you please."

Yes, please, I thought, trying to spot the owner of the voice now that the archers were old news.

The meadow we'd discovered was surrounded by a circle of ancient trees. Their branches had twisted and twined with each other over the years until they grew together in great knots of living wood, joining each tree to its companion.

The canopy of branches grew straight up. Not a single tree grew inside the circle.

"There is magic here," Malachi murmured. "I can smell it. Old magic."

Something pricked my back. I glanced over my shoulder to see more archers--identical to the first twelve.

"There are more archers behind us now," I said. "What should we do?"

"We don't have much of a choice," Jenny said, stepping forward as an archer prodded her back. "We'll have to go where they lead, I suppose." She didn't sound very happy about that prospect.

I wasn't very happy either, but short of a miracle, we were stuck. To find Rianna and get home, we'd have to get past our guards first, and I couldn't think of a way to negotiate with silent wood sprites, or whatever they were. And I still had not spotted the woman who belonged to the voice.

"Do you mind if I take your arm?" Malachi asked, pitching his voice loud enough to be heard. "I have no wish to fall out of step."

I gave him my arm. He clung to it for a moment, as if gathering his strength, and then took a small step forward.

An arrow pricked my back again.

I glared at the archer behind me. "Your mistress never said how long it should take you to bring us to wherever we're going, you know."

In response, the archer prodded my back again. I sighed and stepped up the pace.

We walked in silence across the meadow. Malachi did not release my arm until we stepped through a natural arch between two trees and into the murky light of the forest again.

"I couldn't--*see* back there," he whispered. "Sense, I suppose. I barely smelled our guards. I could have been standing on the edge of a chasm, and I would not have known the danger." He shivered and touched a nearby tree trunk for support.

One of the archers batted his hand away. Malachi growled at him before he could stop himself.

A length of grapevine slithered through the leaves near Malachi's feet. Before I could warn him, it erupted out of the ground, twining around his legs so fast that I barely saw it attack.

He fell back against the tree. Another vine wrapped around his throat. He clawed at it, gasping for air as it tightened.

Jenny lunged forward. One of the archers stepped in her path and she shoved him away, unmindful of the arrows.

Vines writhed across the ground now, snaking up Jenny's legs. They had reached Malachi's waist now, encasing him in a seething mass of vegetation.

I did the only thing I could think of, other than scream. Without a thought to my own safety, I picked up a dead branch from the ground, threw it at the nearest archers, and then grabbed the closest sapling I could find.

"If you don't let them go, I'll kill this tree!" I shouted to the sky.

The furious growth stopped. Not a single leaf rustled, save for those around Malachi's throat as he gasped and struggled.

"Let them go," I said. "Now."

The vines vanished. They didn't snake back into the ground; they just disappeared. Malachi sagged to his knees, his head inches from the ground as he drew in great gulps of air. Jenny knelt next to him, protecting him from the archers who remained on guard.

Some of them had vanished with the vines, I noticed. Had they been the source?

I didn't release the sapling. "We came in peace," I said. "Without any intention of causing you harm. But you have harmed us. You struck the first blow."

"A Hound, a Hag, and a human?" The voice was a mere whisper of its former power. "I believe you not."

I remembered something Jenny had mentioned, long before. "You could truthspell all of us, and you would see what I say is true," I said. "I have no reason to lie to you."

"To save your life, perhaps. Release the tree."

"Show yourself," I ordered. "Give us safe passage."

The voice laughed. "Little human, I am all around you. And I cannot grant what you wish."

I glanced at Malachi. I had no idea what to do, but I had a feeling neither Malachi nor Jenny would be of any help.

"Then I claim this tree's life in payment for the wrong you have done to us," I said, and bent its trunk just enough to make it creak. I didn't really want to kill the tree, but I didn't really want to die, either. I could imagine Penny's reaction to the news of my death, especially with the director gone on vacation.

"No!"

The wind whipped up again, furious now. Leaves and dirt and tiny stones struck my face and hands, but I held tight and squeezed my eyes closed against the onslaught.

"We came here for the child!" Malachi shouted, his voice hoarse. "We came for Rianna!"

The wind, like the vines, vanished. Once more, I shook leaves and twigs out of my hair.

"Who?" Her voice quivered a little, or maybe that was just the wind.

"A little girl," Jenny said. "She's four years old, and her name is Rianna. She talks to trees. We think her mother might have been a dryad."

"A lot of children talk to trees," the woman said.

"But the trees don't usually answer back," Malachi whispered.

Silence reigned for a little while. My hand began to cramp, but I didn't dare let go of the tree. I had no way to tell if the woman--whoever she was-- intended to kill us or hear us out. And this small tree was my only bargaining chip.

"No offence," I whispered to it, feeling a little silly to be talking to a tree. I didn't know *what* I would do if the tree answered back. "I don't really want to kill you."

The wind returned, but it was softer now, curious. It played with Jenny's hair and swept across Malachi's face. It left me alone.

"Your words have the ring of truth," the woman's voice finally said. "If you give me your word, human, that you'll release the tree unharmed, I will give you *my* word that you may proceed safely."

"Call me Karen," I said automatically.

"What?" Now she sounded a bit peeved.

"My name isn't 'human'," I said. "My name is Karen. My companions are Malachi and Jenny, not Hound and Hag." I glanced at Malachi. "Do we want to accept her word?"

Malachi rubbed his throat and allowed Jenny to help him to his feet. "Sure."

I released the tree. "Very well, then."

The tree rustled, shaking its leaves as if it tried to cast away the feel of my hands from its bark.

"Please accept my apologies for the intrusion," I said, and gave it a little bow.

"Proceed," the woman said, unamused. "My archers will guide your way."

We walked down a faint and twisting path choked with weeds and rotting leaves. The forest remained silent, save for the sound of our muffled footsteps. And one by one, the archers melted into the background until there were only four left.

We probably could have overpowered them and taken their weapons, but I had no desire to get on the wrong side of the invisible woman again. Thankfully, neither Jenny nor Malachi seemed to harbor the desire to attack the archers either.

The forest darkened as we walked. Sunlight peeked fitfully through the thick blanket of leaves above us, but it rarely reached the forest floor. There weren't as many seedlings here, or saplings. Most of the trees around us had trunks I could not circle with both arms.

If the forest in the beginning had been virgin forest, this was primeval forest. I would not have been surprised to see a saber-toothed tiger crouched on an overhanging branch. Or a giant sloth. Or even a dinosaur.

"You did well back there," Malachi whispered, slowing so he could walk beside me. "I wouldn't have thought to threaten a tree."

"Research pays off," I said. "Or working in a library pays off. You never know when useless information might come in handy."

In fact, I'd made a wild guess, but he didn't have to know that. In hindsight, my guess made perfect sense. Whatever *that* was worth.

The path branched and widened, becoming well-traveled and broad enough for two people to walk side by side. Our guides slowly melted away as the ancient forest began to subtly shift, becoming the forest I was more used to seeing. I could name some of these trees. Ash. Maple. Pin Oak. Cedar. A dogwood bloomed out of season, a white splash in a medley of browns and greens.

Only one remained when I heard voices up ahead. *Human* voices. Or at least they sounded human to me.

I turned to ask Malachi about the voices just as our last guide vanished into the forest.

"Hey!" I spun around and Malachi was gone, sucked into the forest like he had never existed. Another turn, and Jenny had vanished as well. Both without a protest.

Leaving me alone.

And the voices were getting louder.

I thought about ducking behind a tree off one side of the path, but I hesitated to actually step *off* the path. I'd done that once before in Faerie and nothing bad had happened, but this was not Faerie. Or--at least I didn't think it was Faerie anymore.

A bird trilled somewhere in the forest. I saw a squirrel--the only sign of habitation I'd seen as yet--jump from branch to branch across a small stream twenty feet away.

And the voices grew louder.

There was a bend in the path ten feet away. As I stood and dithered, two hikers walked around the curve, deep into a conversation that had something to do with a guy named Ronald and where he would be sleeping tonight.

They paid no attention to me. In fact, they walked right *through* me before I could move.

I gaped after them as they, too, vanished into thin air.

What was I supposed to do now? In all the stories I'd read--for research, of course--the heroine always had some sort of item that some wizened old woman or a mysterious something-or-other had given her. I had nothing but the clothes on my back and the lint in my pockets. Well, I had my wallet, but credit cards were pretty useless in the wilderness.

I didn't even have a book to read. Which says a lot, if you think about it.

I turned around in a circle, looking for some clue as to what I should do. From what I could tell, I had three choices. Continue walking, go back the way I had come, or step off the path and see what happened.

A large toad hopped out from the underbrush and stopped in the middle of the path. We stared at each other for a moment, and then it opened its mouth.

"Are you a princess?"

I closed my eyes. My mind had finally cracked. "No. I'm not. Sorry."

When I opened my eyes, the toad still sat in the middle of the path.

"Are you *sure* you're not a princess?" it asked.

My smile felt more like a grimace. "Positive. And I don't know any either, before you ask." I. Was. Talking. To. A. *Toad.*

"Oh." If toads could look depressed, this one had it down pat. "Well, sorry to bother you, then." It hopped to the other edge of the path, then glanced at me over its little toad shoulder. "Are you lost?"

"Not exactly." *Why* was I standing on a hiking path in the middle of a forest talking to a toad? "My companions disappeared, and I was trying to decide which way to go."

"Are your companions a Hound and a Water Hag?" the toad asked. "If so, they're standing right behind you, just past that tree."

I had to turn to look. "I don't see them."

"Of course not," the toad said patiently. "That's because you're in *this* world, and they're in the other. The Veil is thin here."

"Well, how do I get back to where they are?" I asked, wondering if this toad was a Council member in disguise. It could have been one, just with its knack for the art of obfuscation.

"Well, you either go back the way you came, continue walking, or step off the path and see what happens, of course," the toad said, and hopped into the forest, leaving me to make my own decision.

"Of course," I muttered, and stepped off the path.

The forest swung around me in a dizzying blur. I stumbled over a root, started to fall, and a hand pulled me back from the edge of a sheer drop that had not been in evidence a second before.

"*This* is not Ohio," Malachi said, after helping me regain my footing.

"You vanished!" I hissed, backing away from the edge. "You both vanished!"

"So did you," Jenny said. "The Veil is very thin here."

"I saw hikers!" I sat down before my legs collapsed and tried to catch my breath. *And a toad that talked to me!* But did I want to make it known that I'd had a conversation with a toad whose first words were to ask if I was a princess? "Where are we and what happened?"

"Look down," Malachi said, pointing to the edge of the cliff.

I crept forward, tensing as I peered over the edge. The gray rocks were slick under my hands. I soon found out why.

A silent waterfall poured from a hole in the rock face of the cliff about twenty feet below us, ending in a pool of deep blue water. Sunlight streamed down from above where the forest ended and the valley began, and the sparkling water reflected the light like a thousand precious jewels.

On the bank of the pool of water grew an immense tree that shadowed the larger trees we'd passed in the forest. Or, perhaps it was just as large, but since it was not crowded close together with many other trees, it just looked larger. Its branches reached up towards the sky and its roots plunged into the pool of water, dark twisting masses that poked up here and there like the undulating coils of a giant snake.

Since there were no visible streams leading away from the pool, I had no idea where all the water went, unless the tree needed that much water to survive.

"What kind of a tree is that?" I whispered. The leaves were too far below for me to make out any detail of their shape or size.

"I can't tell from this far up," Jenny said. "It could be oak or ash, from its size, but if we're in Faerie, it could be just about anything."

"Look beyond," Malachi said.

I let my gaze travel past the tree, to where a circle of trees grew--an identical circle to the one we'd discovered before. Only this time, there were no archers, and no other trees grew around their twisting forms.

"I can't sense anything beyond the beginning of the path," Malachi whispered.

When I turned my head, I noticed a narrow path that twisted along one side of the cliff. From above, it looked to be only inches wide in spots.

"We aren't going down that path, are we?" I croaked, appalled.

"I don't believe we have much of a choice," Jenny said.

"Why isn't the Council here?" It was one thing to risk my life for a little girl, but when there were wizards who were much more capable--and trained--for dealing with magic, I saw no reason why they shouldn't be standing on the edge of a cliff in my place.

"What do you mean?" Malachi asked.

"Has anyone ever noticed how the Council seems to let everyone else do the work, and then reap the rewards after everything is said and done?" I stared down at the path. "This is ridiculous."

Malachi laughed. "You volunteered to come," he reminded me. "And the Council cannot risk losing one of its members, since they are so few. That's why they--delegate so often."

"Yes, well." I sighed. "If we have to go down the path, then we have to go down the path. But if I die, I want one of you to bury me back in the forest."

Malachi cocked his head. "Not at the library?"

"No. The forest will haunt my dreams more than the library ever will," I said. "And the library already has a resident ghost."

The ground rumbled beneath us. I grabbed hold of the nearest hand--Malachi's, in this instance--and scrambled backwards, away from the edge.

"Maybe not, if there are earthquakes involved." Somehow, the prospect of falling into that pool from a hundred feet up did not excite me in any way, shape, or form.

Jenny peeked over the edge. "Well, that's interesting."

I didn't want to get too close, just in case another earthquake caught us by surprise. "What?"

"There are steps now. Not just a path." She turned around. "Perhaps the ground agrees with your wish to be buried here."

Malachi's hand tightened in mine. "I still can't sense anything."

"Well, *I* can't hear anything," I said. "Shouldn't that waterfall make a lot of noise?"

"You're right. It should." Malachi shook his head. "It could be a trick. Or an illusion."

"Or perhaps we haven't passed through that part of the Veil just yet," Jenny said. "What we're seeing might be what lies at the bottom of the cliff, or it could be something else entirely."

"That's reassuring," I said, struggling to keep the sarcasm out of my voice. It had been a *long* day already, and it wasn't over yet. Creating a proposal for the new library branches was a piece of cake compared to this. "But it would explain why Malachi can't sense anything."

"True," Malachi murmured, his sightless eyes unfocused. He blinked and raised his head. "Shall we go, then? I'll need someone to guide me down."

Jenny volunteered, leaving me the unenviable position of leader.

Twenty-seven steps down, the roar of the waterfall eclipsed the frantic beating of my heart. As we descended, the steps grew slippery with mould and water. Faint spray from the waterfall lashed our bodies, washing away the remnants of the wind's fury back in the forest.

Fifty-four steps down, Malachi slipped, but Jenny caught him before he could fall. Seventy-three steps down, the water evaporated in the face of blinding sunlight, leaving us wet and miserable as we trudged down the rest of the steps.

One hundred and three steps, to be exact. And at the bottom, a large long stretch of flat stone had settled, warmed by the sun and surrounded by water on three sides.

I sank to my knees and used a relatively clean edge of my shirt to wipe the sweat from my face. "At least we weren't walking *up* the stairs." At least I'd worn comfortable clothing and sensible shoes to work that morning. At least I hadn't given in to the siren call of the warm weather and worn a skirt.

Even Malachi and Jenny looked a bit worse for wear, although Jenny had obviously found some sort of refreshment from the waterfall's spray. Sometime between the first step and the last, her dress had repaired itself, and now sported filmy blue patches here and there, seamlessly molded with the original fabric.

Malachi's clothes were just muddy and wet, as were mine. He wiped his face and stared around us, obviously searching for some sign of a path.

"We're standing on rock," I said to be helpful. "As far as I can tell, we're surrounded on three sides by water."

The lumpy brown roots from the tree across the pond drew my gaze. "Although--we might be able to get across if we use the roots as stepping stones."

"*You* might be able to get across," Malachi said. "Considering I can't *see* these roots of yours, I'll have to find another way."

Jenny gave the distance between the shore and our peninsula a considering glance. "I might be able to jump across it if I have enough space for a running start."

"And if you don't have enough space?" Even though she hadn't tried to drown me before, we hadn't really been in contact with enough water for a good drowning. The pool, although shallow, would do the trick quite well.

Jenny hesitated. "Then I swim for it."

"Have you ever swum with passengers and not tried to drown them?" Malachi was channeling Gabriel again, his voice as calm as a windless day.

"Well." Jenny wouldn't look at either of us. "No. Have you ever disobeyed your Master as a Hound?"

"No. Not as a Hound." Malachi stood for a moment, lost in thought. "I'll go first, then. If you drown me, then Karen will know she has to find a different way across."

I gaped at him. "What? If she drowns you, you'll be dead!"

"Yes, that's true." Malachi didn't seem to be very worried at the prospect. "However, *you'll* still be alive. I trust you'll continue on."

"But--" But what? It was his decision, and he was an adult. Or as close as an adult as a member of the Wild Hunt could be. I did not relish the idea of returning home without him, though. Gabriel would be furious. To say the least.

Jenny swallowed hard. "Are you sure you want to do this?"

"This may be the only way," Malachi whispered. "I trust you, Jenny."

"I am honored by your trust," Jenny said. "I only hope I can trust myself." She shifted before either of us could reply, and backed away from the pool until her tail hit stone.

I didn't see how she would be able to jump so far with so little space to get a running start. I moved away to give her room to maneuver, and sat down on the second-to-last step.

I wasn't a religious person, but I clasped my hands and prayed. I did *not* want to lose Malachi. And I definitely didn't want to face Jenny if he *did* drown.

Malachi had no trouble mounting. He took hold of her mane and pulled himself up onto her back, outwardly calm, even now.

"Good luck," I said, and meant it with all my heart. And then, as Jenny's hooves struck stone, I covered my eyes, because I didn't have enough courage to watch.

Almost immediately, I forced my hands away from my face, because if there's one thing a librarian can't stand, it's not knowing what happens next.

Jenny bolted to the edge of the peninsula, gathered her strength, and leapt into the air. Even from where I sat, I could see that her leap would fall far short of the bank on the other side. But she must have known she would not make it. She landed neatly on a flattened knot of roots and leaped again, straining her entire body to make it to the other side.

Her front hooves landed on the grassy bank. Her back end sank into the water. She neighed, struggling madly to climb up the side, but the pool must have been deeper than I thought. Jenny slid backwards with Malachi still on her back, and vanished under the water.

I ran to the edge of the pool. A second later, a Hound's head popped up above the water, but of course he had no idea which way to go.

"Left!" I shouted, feeling utterly useless on shore. "Swim to your left!"

Malachi turned and dog-paddled to the opposite bank. He had no trouble pulling himself up, using the knotted roots as footholds. He shook himself, letting water fly everywhere, and shifted into human form.

"Where's Jenny?" He took one step forward, began to slide, and fell back.

"She hasn't come up yet," I said, trying to see into the depths of the pool. The sun's reflection made it difficult to see any details more than six inches from the surface. "I can't see her."

"She didn't fall in on purpose," Malachi said. "I felt something brush my leg." He hesitated. "Can you swim?"

"Not very well," I hazarded, still trying to see into the depths of the water. Surely he didn't intend to suggest that I dive in to rescue Jenny, who was to water like I was to books. "Wait a second--" Was that something moving down below? I backed away from the edge as the dark shape grew larger and larger, headed straight towards me.

"Karen?" Malachi must have felt helpless, standing on the other side of the bank with no way to come to my aid. "Karen, what's happening?"

"I'm not sure," I said, inching forward as something *glooped* to the surface of the pool. I saw filmy garments, first, trailing blood into the water. A human shaped hand, but with three-inch-long fingernails, filed into points. Black hair drifted from the body like rotten seaweed. Before my numb mind could react to the fact that this creature wasn't our missing Water Hag, Jenny pulled herself out of the water and wrung out her hair, none the worse for wear.

"Well." Jenny stood and took a deep breath. "Since Kelpies are notorious loners, I don't think we'll have any problems when I take you across."

I stared at her, then at the body. "That's a Kelpie?"

"Yes." Her lip curled. "She tried to drown me. Drown me! *Me!*" She raised her head and searched until she spotted Malachi on the opposite bank. "Your trust in me was well-placed, Malachi. Thank you."

Malachi smiled as a cloud dimmed the sun far above us. "No, thank *you.*"

By the time Jenny carried me across, thunder had dimmed the roar of the waterfall. Lightning flashed among the clouds, but the rain did not begin to fall until we had walked past the immense tree--an oak, Jenny said--and started up the low rise to where the circle of trees waited.

The previous heat from the sun was but a memory now as icy rain pasted our clothes to our skin. I could not tell if this was a magical storm or a mundane one, but when the wind howled down the side of the cliff and sent a wave of water rushing up the hill, I realized the screaming I heard wasn't just from the wind.

"Aren't there rules in place for times like these?" I shouted to Jenny as she struggled up the incline. What had seemed a low hill had turned into a mud-slicked slide; too slick to climb up without the support of a good walking stick.

"What do you mean?"

Malachi fell to his knees and shifted shape, struggling up the hill in the form of a Hound, his eyes narrowed in concentration.

I lost my shoes to the sucking mud, one right after the other. Since my socks were already wet, I pulled them off and dug my toes into slimy, vicious ooze as I struggled to stay on my feet.

"Rules!" I shouted. "We've fought through every single obstacle in our path! We were assured safe passage! And we can't even get up this damn hill!"

I don't curse very often, and my vocabulary of curse words usually contain more than one syllable. However, this latest deluge had driven me to the brink of insanity. If this kept up, I'd start lecturing about the inherent literary qualities of the *Sports Illustrated* swimsuit edition.

Malachi shifted, up to his knees and elbows in mud. "The only rule is that the harder it gets to go on, the closer you are to your goal."

I gritted my teeth. Whether it be an obscure reference question or a mud-slicked hill, librarians *never* give up.

By the time we reached the top, I was too out of breath and dripping wet to care that the storm had subsided. Malachi, now more brown than white, tried to shake some of the mud from his fur, but that only made it stick up in wet clumps, giving him the look of a particularly irritated porcupine. Jenny was the only one of us who had been washed clean by the rain. Although her feet and the hem of her dress were muddy, she thrived on all the water.

I, on the other hand, feared that my fingers and toes would never be the same again.

Before I could hesitate, I squelched to the edge of the circle of trees. As the clouds broke away above us, sunlight shimmered across the valley again, illuminating the inside of the circle. There were no archers waiting for us this time.

In fact, the circle was empty.

I turned towards Malachi and Jenny. "This is really too much. My feet hurt, my head hurts, and I'm soaking wet. And we don't even know if Rianna is here!"

"I *did* tell you I knew of no Rianna," the woman's voice said. It lacked the eerie quality of before. In fact, it sounded like she stood right behind me. Which made perfect sense, of course, in horror stories, but *I* was no stupid heroine.

I turned around anyway, determined to show no surprise. "No, actually you didn't tell us anything of the sort."

The woman who stood with one hand on the rough bark of the nearest tree had flowing nut-brown hair and a definite green tint to her skin. Her lips were the palest of pinks, her eyes as dark as night. She wore a white gown that shimmered as she walked towards us, like a spider-web on a summer morning after a heavy dew.

"A Hound, a Hag and a human." Her voice was low and musical. "Truly I did not expect you to come so far for so little." She smiled. "I do not know this child, Rianna. She is not here."

"Four years ago, a child was born to a human and a girl who vanished into the forest a week after the baby was born," I said. "This little girl talks to trees, and they talk back."

"That is not my concern," the woman said. "Perhaps she met with misfortune from a--more *local* source." She glared at Jenny as she spoke, leaving her words open to only one interpretation.

Jenny shook her head. "I don't think so. Rianna's a very special little girl. And she has a loving father who cares for her very much."

"Where is he, then?" the woman asked. "I don't see her *father* risking life and limb to save her."

She had a good point, but I bet I could guess why that particular issue was never raised.

"Because her father is human, and he doesn't know a thing about magic," I said. "And I doubt the Council would have let him come. As far as he's concerned, Rianna's mother abandoned her daughter and what chance they all had at a life together."

I had no idea if the picture in my pocket had survived the trip, but I carefully removed it and unfolded Rianna's drawing.

"But somehow, Rianna knew about her mother." I held the wet paper across both hands in full view of everyone. "I don't know how. Maybe the trees told her. Maybe she figured it out on her own."

The woman's gaze fastened on the piece of paper. As she moved forward, away from the circle, the trees nearest to us sighed as a light breeze played through their leaves.

"Where did you get this?" She extended one finger to trace the crayoned *Mommy*.

"On a bulletin board in her daycare," I said. "It's a very good daycare, and she probably didn't need vaccinations or medical records to attend. But next year, she'll be starting kindergarten, and there might be questions if the school officials find out she's not exactly human."

"She will learn everything she needs to know here," the woman said, her gaze still fixed on Rianna's drawing.

I didn't have enough strength to exchange triumphant glances with Malachi or Jenny, but I saw Malachi's fierce grin out of the corner of my eye.

"And what will happen when she grows up? What will happen when she discovers she's not fully of *your* world, either?"

"She--" the woman took one step backwards. "This is the best way. For everyone involved."

"Leaving her father to mourn her as dead?" Malachi asked. "We found the changeling, milady. The Council has it now. They know what it is, and they will not rest until Rianna is returned--safely--to her father."

The woman's lip curled. "The *Council.* Meddling wizards. And why aren't *they* here?"

"Because we volunteered to come," Jenny said. "I know Rianna's father. He must be heartbroken and frantic with worry."

"He was a good man," the woman whispered. "But we have no children here. I cannot let her go." She swept out her arm, indicating the valley around us. "Once our children grew here undisturbed. Nurtured by our Mother the oak, with their roots digging deep in this soil. But there are no children anymore. Just Rianna." She turned away from us and stepped into the circle. "Surely you understand."

"But doesn't Rianna's father have any say in her upbringing?" I asked.

"He had my daughter for four years," the woman whispered. "I could not wait any longer." She vanished into the glare of sunlight.

"Wait!" Malachi stepped forward, his hands outstretched. "Please. There must be another way to end this. We cannot return and tell him of his beloved daughter's death."

I wracked my brain for an answer that would satisfy both parents. Something that would give Rianna the best of both worlds. There were plenty of separated or divorced parents around, after all. They had to raise their children somehow.

"Wait!" I ran to the edge of the trees. Rianna's mother hadn't walked far. "There might be a way to make this work!"

She turned to face me. "How?"

"In my world, it's called joint custody," I said. "That way Rianna could be raised with the best of both worlds."

"*Both* worlds?" The woman laughed. "Impossible. Humans exist to destroy what they do not understand. The stress alone would kill her."

"Not necessarily," I said. "It works quite well in most cases. Both parents have a say. Both parents can raise their child or children. And no one feels as if their son or daughter has been torn from their lives forever."

"You did say he was a good man," Jenny reminded her.

"He was," the woman said. "Four years ago. And he would never agree to such a thing. He is human."

"But he loves his daughter," Malachi said. "And there's only one way to find out if he would agree to the arrangement or not."

"What way?" her voice softened.

"All I have to do is ask my Master to contact him, and he could be here," Malachi said. "If he truly loves his daughter, he will come."

The woman hesitated. "Do you think he *would* come?"

"I would bet on it," Jenny said.

"Then contact your Master," the woman said after a long moment of thought. "And we shall see if he agrees to this--'joint custody' of yours."

Malachi only spent a moment in silent communication with Gabriel, but that moment was enough for me to wonder if he *had* asked Gabriel's permission after all. He didn't quite cringe as he stood there, but he came very close.

He rubbed his temples as he walked back to where we waited. "My Master has agreed to bring him here. I trust they will have an easier journey?"

The woman made a dismissive gesture with one hand. "There is a--hiking trail at the top of the cliff that passes through the Veil. Instruct him to take that route." Her voice dropped. "That was the route I took when I met Rianna's father."

"The high road and the low road," I muttered. "Do you suppose Lucas knew there was an easier way to get here?"

"I hope not," Malachi growled.

A whole twenty minutes later, Gabriel appeared at the top of the cliff with a young man in tow. The waterfall slowed to a trickle as they descended--of course--and by the time they reached the bottom, a solid bridge of roots had grown to stretch from the peninsula to the opposite shore.

Even the mud had mysteriously vanished by the time they approached the circle.

Malachi quivered as his Master approached. "You wouldn't have given me permission to go," he said before Gabriel could speak.

I stared at him with renewed respect. It took a lot of courage--especially for a Hound--to not only do something like this without Gabriel's knowledge, but also hide it from the bond that connected the Hunt at all times.

Gabriel stared at him, his eyes narrowed. "No, I wouldn't have."

Malachi's nostrils flared. "I had to go. To know, myself, if I could."

Gabriel did not speak. In fact, the silence stretched on for so long that I thought Rianna's mother had frozen them somehow.

"Malachi is very brave," I said, trying to help.

"Telling stories to children is a bit different than risking your life for the sake of a child," Gabriel said softly, ignoring me.

Beside him, Rianna's father stared at both Master and Hound. "I thought you said you had information about my daughter?" His voice cracked on the last word.

Malachi raised his chin. "I would have done the same for Eri. Or any other child. I am not helpless." He paid no mind to Rianna's father.

"No. I do." The woman in white appeared again, one hand resting on a tree trunk. "Hello, Kyle."

"I realize that," Gabriel said. "And I will not make that mistake again."

I was beginning to have a hard time keeping track of all the conversations.

Rianna's father blinked at her. "M-Maire? But I--you--you *vanished*!" He ran one hand through tousled hair and blinked at her with the red-rimmed eyes of the newly bereaved.

"Thank you, my lord," Malachi said, smiling.

"This is my home," Maire said, her voice sad now. "These trees are my home."

Kyle licked his lips. "Your home. I don't understand."

"The Council is going to *love* this," Malachi murmured.

Maire held out her hand. "Come with me. I'll try to explain."

They vanished into the trees, awash in sunlight. A moment later, I heard Kyle shout, and a little voice cry, "Daddy!"

Gabriel folded his arms and leaned against a tree. "Don't *ever* assume I will forbid you again, Malachi. I would much rather discover you disobeyed than come across your body at the foot of a cliff."

I sat on the ground and tried to scrub the worst of the mud from between my toes. "He really *did* intend to tell stories to the children Jenny takes care of," I said, remembering Mrs. Green with a sharp pang. I would miss the old lady. She'd always brought a certain amount of--brightness into my day.

Jenny regarded the Master of the Hunt with a certain amount of wariness, no doubt remembering the Hunt's closeness to the Council.

"Yes, he did." She hesitated. "He also swore that the Council would not find out about my part in this."

"And what is your part in this?" Gabriel asked. "I can smell what you are. And I have killed your kind before."

Jenny squared her shoulders and stood in front of him, her hands clenched. "I know you have. But we've changed. I run a daycare now, right outside of Amington."

"I thought that daycare was run by an older--woman," Gabriel said mildly.

Jenny gaped at him. "You *knew* about us?"

"I know about you, yes," Gabriel said. "And you needn't fear that I or my Hunt will call the Council down upon you. We are no longer bound to serve them."

"Aunt Janet decided to go into the fire," Jenny said. "Leaving me in charge." She still regarded Gabriel with suspicion, as if she couldn't quite bring herself to believe his words.

But Gabriel did not recant, or condemn her.

And Malachi shifted, curled up at his Master's feet, and fell asleep.

The sun had just set when Kyle and Maire appeared with Rianna between them.

"We have decided to try this 'joint custody' arrangement," Maire said, smiling at me. "Thank you for the suggestion. It might truly be the best of both worlds."

Rianna beamed when she saw Jenny, and tugged at her father's hand.

"Jenny is a fairy princess," she whispered, loud enough for everyone to hear.

Kyle had the look of a newly baptized member of the other side. He stared at Jenny. "Are you really?" Obviously, after discovering that his daughter's mother was a dryad, the poor guy was ready to believe anything.

"Not exactly," she said, but didn't elaborate.

I hoped he didn't ask Gabriel or Malachi about their supernatural origins. I didn't think he could handle the Wild Hunt.

He stared at me. "And what are you? Some sort of guardian angel?"

"No, actually I'm a librarian," I said, which truly explained everything.

We left them there, this newfound family, to work out the custody arrangements in peace. And we took the shortcut home. Although, in truth, I wouldn't have minded the trek back through the forest.

After bidding Jenny goodbye, giving Lucas a report that made no mention of her presence, and leaving Malachi and his Master to make their way home, I drove back to my apartment and mundane life.

Life slowly returned to our version of normal. I dragged myself into work on Tuesday, and somehow made it through the rest of the week. The weekend passed in a blur of facts and figures as Ivy delivered even more reports to my front door.

Monday morning dawned and Penny beat me to work by an hour. By Tuesday, I was so deep in spreadsheets that my eyes played tricks on me every time I glanced away from the computer screen.

At three thirty-five Tuesday afternoon, Penny's voice burst through the intercom on my phone.

"Ms. Montgomery?"

I had only closed my eyes for a moment, but there was an awfully large puddle of drool on my desk. Before I replied, I took a sip of lukewarm tea, closed my aching eyes, and rubbed my temples.

"Yes?"

"There's--someone here to see you," Penny said. "The same person who came here a week and a half ago. He had a strange name, but I can't remember his name."

"Malachi," I said. What was strange about the name Malachi?

"He said he wanted to see you, if you have a minute to spare," Penny said.

"I always have a minute for Malachi," I said. "Go ahead and send him back. He knows the way."

A minute later, Malachi knocked on my door. I'd cleared the pile of papers from my visitor's chair, but I didn't have enough room to do much about the rest of my mess.

"I apologize for disturbing you," he said before I could speak. "Penny told me you were very busy. But I thought--well, Gabriel said it wouldn't hurt to ask."

"What do you need?" I turned off my computer monitor for the first time in days and gave him my full attention. "He didn't--" Dared I ask? "Gabriel didn't punish you, did he?"

"No." Malachi flushed. "He--said he was proud of me." He still seemed faintly amazed.

My heart warmed a bit towards the Master of the Hunt. "I'm happy to hear that. I *did* wonder."

"Maybe he *has* truly changed, and us with him," Malachi said. "That's why I came, in truth." He hesitated. "You said--you said Jenny's aunt brought the children on Tuesdays and Thursdays."

And today was Tuesday. "Right. And they should be back with Jenny now, so I expect they'll be arriving soon." Why was he asking? Did he want me to give Jenny a message? Or, perhaps--and then I knew, just like that. I almost gave him my blessing right then and there, but on second thought, decided to wait and see if he would ever get around to asking.

"Do you suppose--" He sighed. "It's still difficult to ask for something for myself."

"I'm not your Master," I said. "I'm just a librarian. And I'm not going to kick you out of the library for asking a question. Librarians *like* questions." I smiled to put him at ease, then remembered he could not see my smile. But I knew he could *hear* it, even then. "Ask away, Malachi. I won't bite you."

"Would it be permissible for me to tell the children a story today?" Malachi asked.

"Surely you don't still think you're a bad person," I chided, but gently. "Anyone who would risk their life for the sake of a child is not a bad person, unless they do it for all the wrong reasons."

"Yes. I realize that now," Malachi said, bowing his head. "You helped me see, and I am in your debt for that."

"You're not in my debt," I said, knowing how much it had cost him to say that. "You're not the only one who learned something last Monday." Although it seemed I'd already forgotten some of what I learned, if I was still waffling over the proposal I had to create. Perhaps I was approaching the project in the wrong direction. "And I would be very pleased if you told the children a story today."

Malachi's head rose. "You would?" His lips twitched, almost stretching into a smile. "Oh, thank you." Another hesitation. "This means--this means a lot to me."

"Do you mind if I listen in?" I needed some time away from facts and figures. "I promise I'll stay in the back and out of your way."

"I don't mind." His shy smile stretched into a grin. "It's almost time for them to come, isn't it?"

I glanced at my clock. "We have about five minutes. Are you ready to go?"

Malachi took a deep breath. "As ready as I'll ever be."

We walked together through the hallway that separated the main library from Administration. As we emerged at the beginning of the Dewey Decimal system, I saw a line of children file into the meeting room. Jenny was the last in line, wearing another gauzy dress, but with her thick hair plaited into a braid.

Rianna held her hand, looking none the worse for wear.

I had heard--from Ivy, of course--that the Council had approved the unusual custody arrangement without much in the way of protest. Or, as

Lucas had put it--again, by way of Ivy, who seemed to know everything--perhaps Rianna would grow up to study ecology or something, and discover the reason why the dryads were unable to have children.

I thought his reasoning was sound, all things considered.

"They're here, aren't they?" Malachi looked like he wanted to turn tail and run, but he squared his shoulders and stepped forward.

I took his arm. He stiffened and started to pull away, but checked himself at the last minute.

"You'll be fine," I said, and together we walked across the main floor to the meeting room.

He was more than fine. Malachi's story--a tale about a little girl named Eri who had to brave many obstacles to rescue her friend from the clutches of an evil cat-headed creature--received the first standing ovation I'd ever seen at a library program.

With only a tiny amount of begging, I got him to agree to return to do a program in the evening for both children and adults.

Somehow, after watching the way he started to relax as he got deeper and deeper into the tale, the prospect of crafting a proposal to take in front of the board no longer frightened me. And I fully intended to ask, and receive, funding for a room consisting of nothing but books on folklore, myths, and legends. *Someone* had to bridge the gap between both worlds, even if the Council hoped that bridge would never exist.

And since no one else seemed to want the job, that someone would be me.

The end

You can find ALL our books on our website at:

http://www.writers-exchange.com

All Jennifer's books:

http://www.writers-exchange.com/Jennifer-St-Clair/

all our fantasy novels:

http://www.writers-exchange.com/category/genres/fantasy/

About the Author

Jennifer St. Clair grew up in Southern Ohio and spent most of her childhood in the woods around her home. She wrote her first novel when she was thirteen, and hasn't stopped since. She lives with her ball python, Fester, and two cats, Ash and Rowan.

In her spare time, she crochets, makes cloth dolls, collects antiques, books, and vintage clothing, and takes digital photographs with varying degrees of success.

Her *Beth-Hill series* is set in the area in America that contains many supernatural creatures: Wild Hunt, Vampires, Dragons, Faery and more.

It is part of the Universe that her *Jacob Lane Series, Karen Montgomery Series* and vampire trilogy, *The Shadow Series* are set in.

Follow all her books on her author page:

http://www.writers-exchange.com/Jennifer-St-Clair/

If you want to read more about other books by this author, they are listed on the following pages...

A Beth-Hill Novel (Stand Alone Novels)

Are creatures of the night and all manner of extramundane beings drawn to certain locations in the natural world? In the Midwestern village of Beth-Hill located in southern Ohio, the population is made up of its fair share of common citizens...and much more than its share of supernatural residents. Take a walk on the wild side in this unusual place where imagination meets reality.

Blood of Innocents

Ten years ago, Orien, crown prince of the Seleighe, was captured by his mortal enemies, locked in a dungeon and turned into a vampire. Six years into Orien's sentence, the Healer's brother Cullen disobeyed his mistress's orders to kill him and turned him into a vampire instead, thus sealing both their fates for all eternity.

Now both Orien and Cullen are set free. But a secret only Cullen knows lies locked inside his mind, threatening to drive him mad before he can uncover the identity of a traitor--the very elf who betrayed Orien and left them both to die in darkness.

Publisher: http://www.writers-exchange.com/blood-of-innocents/

Full Moon

Werewolves change into wolves when the moon is full. But Edward's curse only allows him to be *human* when the moon is full.

Alone and despairing, Edward hides himself away from the world. He's scraped out a meager existence for himself for almost a century in the forest he's grown to love and call home. But in the depths of a terrible winter, he stumbles across clues from the life his mother left behind in Faerie. The truth may give him the answers he needs about the source of his birthright... and the curse that holds him captive.

Publisher: http://www.writers-exchange.com/full-moon/

A Beth-Hill Novel: Jacob Lane Series

Are creatures of the night and all manner of extramundane beings drawn to certain locations in the natural world? In the Midwestern village of Beth-Hill located in southern Ohio, the population is made up of its fair share of common citizens...and much more than its share of supernatural residents.

Jacob Lane is a ten-year-old girl who's spent her life unaware of her magical heritage. After being sent to Darkbrook, a school of magic, supernatural mysteries seem to spring to life all around her and her new friends.

Book 1: The Tenth Ghost

After Jacob Lane's parents mysteriously vanish, she's sent to Darkbrook, the only school of magic in the United States. While there, she and her new friends stumble upon a series of mysterious deaths in the nine ghosts that haunt the halls of Darkbrook. These ghosts were students who died at the school over the past hundred years. Will Jacob become the tenth ghost, or can she stop a witch's reign of terror?

Publisher: http://www.writers-exchange.com/the-tenth-ghost/

Book 2: The Ninth Guest

When Jacob's friend Ophelia's family decides to open up their castle for guests, amateur paranormal sleuth Jacob Lane is invited to join in on the fun. "Spend the night in a vampire's castle and live to tell the tale!" is supposed to be a fundraiser to help Ophelia's family pay the bills. Heating a castle costs quite a bit, after all. But, after the truth of an old secret is uncovered, what began as an innocent business venture soon turns deadly when vampire hunters get involved.

For years, the vampire hunters have had only one goal: To destroy all vampires. With the help of a new friend, Jacob and Ophelia must work together to save the entire VonBriggle family from extinction.

Publisher: http://www.writers-exchange.com/the-ninth-guest/

Book 3: The Eighth Room

For two hundred years, the Selkies have kept themselves separate from those who live on land. But now the Selkies need allies or they'll be crushed by their ancient enemies, the Finfolk.

Jacob and Ophelia, students at the only school of magic in the United States, uncover a mystery that dates back to Darkbrook's beginnings. While helping clean out old storage rooms for classroom expansion, they find something that might save the Selkies from extinction. With the help of the youngest member of the Wild Hunt who are no longer so wild or terrifying, they must foil the Finfolk who desire the Selkie's destruction...or die trying.

Publisher: http://www.writers-exchange.com/the-eighth-room/

Book 4: The Seventh Secret

After a picture of Niklas, the dragons' liaison to the only school of magic in the United States, shows up in too many newspapers to count, Darkbrook is forced to go on the defensive. The secret of Darkbrook's existence has been discovered. But there are more than dragonhunters in the forest, and, as Jacob Lane, supernatural sleuth and student at Darkbrook, learns how to use her newly discovered talent of healing, she helps to right an old wrong and must battle a teenaged wizard intent on proving--once and for all--that magic is real.

Publisher: http://www.writers-exchange.com/the-seventh-secret/

Book 5: The Sixth Stone

Jacob Lane, supernatural sleuth, and Danny, her werewolf friend, stumble across an alternate world where the Wild Hunt was never bound, and Darkbrook, the school of magic they attend, was abandoned a hundred years ago.

But when the Hounds of the Hunt wish to surrender, the two students are swept up in a whirlwind of heartbreak, betrayal, and the discovery of a lost treasure.

Publisher: http://www.writers-exchange.com/the-sixth-stone/

A Beth-Hill Novella: Karen Montgomery Series

Are creatures of the night and all manner of extramundane beings drawn to certain locations in the natural world? In the Midwestern village of Beth-Hill located in southern Ohio, the population is made up of its fair share of common citizens...and much more than its share of supernatural residents. Take a walk on the wild side in this unusual place where imagination meets reality.

Karen Montgomery was an ordinary woman until she stumbled into the extraordinary... A bargain with elves worth its weight in gold. A plague of sinister ladybugs. Rogue vampire hunters, including one who tries to turn over a new leaf--with disastrous consequences. A ghostly huntsmen of the Wild Hunt wishing for redemption. Karen's life will never be the same again.

Book 1: Budget Cuts

Karen Montgomery is used to taking care of the unpleasant jobs no one else wants to deal with. When a shortage of funds forces her to fire fifteen employees from the library, she isn't happy, but the nasty task has to be done and she is, after all, the boss. But Karen finds finishing her task impossible when she can't seem to track down Ivy Bedinghaus, a night clerk she's never actually met. Once she finally does confront Ivy, she's thrust into a centuries-old conflict that makes her previous troubles radically pale in comparison.

Publisher: http://www.writers-exchange.com/budget-cuts/

Book 2: The Secret of Redemption

Karen Montgomery, librarian, finds herself embroiled in another otherworldly adventure...

A member of the Wild Hunt--ghostly myths that aren't so ghostly (or myth-like) anymore--needs help in reconciling who he once was in life and who he is now.

A little girl has gone missing. And the one most likely responsible for her disappearance is the one Karen must prove innocent.

Publisher: http://www.writers-exchange.com/the-secret-of-redemption/

Book 3: Ladybug, Ladybug

An innocent attempt to rid the library of a plague of ladybugs turns sinister when a rogue vampire hunter gets the contract for pest control.

Ivy Bedinghaus, who works for Karen as a night clerk--along with all the vampires in Beth-Hill--are in danger, and their only hope for survival is with the help of Karen, a member of the Wild Hunt, and Russell Moore, a reformed vampire hunter.

Publisher: http://www.writers-exchange.com/ladybug-ladybug/

Book 4: Detour

One wrong turn sends Karen down a road that shouldn't exist, to the site of an old accident and an even older mystery. With reformed vampire hunter Russell Moore's help, Karen finds the key to the mystery. But Russ keeps his own secrets...some of which are deadly.

When old friends from Russ' past come to call, Karen realizes his secrets might just mean his doom. After a terrible incident three years ago, before Karen met him, Russ wants only to live the rest of his life quietly in Beth-Hill. But his secret might not allow him the new lease on life Russ longs for.

Publisher: http://www.writers-exchange.com/detour/

Companion Story: Russ' Story: Capture

Long before Russell Moore ever met supernatural sleuth Karen Montgomery or set foot in Beth-Hill, he was a vampire hunter, possibly the best vampire hunter of all. He brought down whole nests of vampires, caring little about the consequences of his actions. Anyone who lived with or helped the vampires became enemies to be slaughtered.

So what kind of an idiot would capture a ruthless vampire hunter without a conscience and try to reform him?

Ethan Walker was that idiot. Wanting to protect his family, Ethan set out to prove to Russ that vampires weren't all evil, soulless creatures. If Russ would allow himself to witness their lives, see their humanity, surely he and other vampire hunters like him would let them live in peace. *Surely?*

Publisher: http://www.writers-exchange.com/capture/

Secrets When in Shadow Lie

Twelve years ago, Ryan Grey was cursed by a witch to hide a secret. He's lived with the curse of being unable to die permanently, and, over the years he's slowly losing the memory of his past until almost nothing remains.

But now, after a chance meeting with an elf named Zipporah, he discovers the key to unlocking the secret and breaking the curse once and for all...if he can survive the breaking.

Publisher: http://www.writers-exchange.com/secrets-when-in-shadow-lie/

The Dead Who Do Not Sleep

Will Spark only wants a good night's sleep after a night of drinking. Instead, two thugs bang on his door, demanding answers to questions he can't understand. And then they killed him...

Publisher: http://www.writers-exchange.com/the-dead-who-do-not-sleep/

A Beth-Hill Novel: The Abby Duncan Series

Are creatures of the night and all manner of extramundane beings drawn to certain locations in the natural world? In the Midwestern village of Beth-Hill located in southern Ohio, the population is made up of its fair share of common citizens...and much more than its share of supernatural residents. Take a walk on the wild side in this unusual place where imagination meets reality.

Situated in Beth-Hill, where imagination meets reality, is The Rose Emporium, owned by elderly and not-a-little-odd Rose Duncan. The large Victorian house smackdab in the middle of nowhere is a cross between a pawn shop and an antique store that caters to supernatural creatures needing to barter. Rose's twenty-something niece, Abby Duncan, discovers that the world isn't made up of just run-of-the-mill, ordinary humans but an entire spectrum of unusual beings. With her preconceptions about what's normal and what's not turned upside-down, Abby is in for a whole lot of startling truths, mysteries-- about herself and the people and places around her--and danger.

Novella 1: By Any Other Name

Woodturner Abby Duncan decides to sell her spindles at a local Renaissance Festival with only some success. After all, no one really spins their own yarn anymore, do they? While there, she discovers that one of her newfound friends is not what he appears--and his secret is about to get him killed!

Publisher: http://www.writers-exchange.com/by-any-other-name/

Book 2: The Uncrowned Queen

Abby Duncan's elderly Aunt Rose has always been a bit odd. And now she's off on a mysterious trip, leaving Abby behind to run the Rose Emporium, an unusual sort of antique shop. Such an extraordinary store would have been a perfect place for Seth and the others, her friends from the Renaissance Festival, to take a break from traveling between Faires. But when tragedy strikes and Abby and the others discover the true nature of the Rose Emporium, they'll have to travel into Faerie itself before their tightknit group is whole again.

Abby doesn't know much about her family history, but she's about to find out the truth...whether she likes it or not.

Publisher: http://www.writers-exchange.com/the-uncrowned-queen/

Book 3: Coming Soon!

A Beth-Hill Novel: The Shadows Trilogy

Are creatures of the night and all manner of extramundane beings drawn to certain locations in the natural world? In the Midwestern village of Beth-Hill located in southern Ohio, the population is made up of its fair share of common citizens...and much more than its share of supernatural residents. Take a walk on the wild side in this unusual place where imagination meets reality.

A Dreamer dreams the future when the past is not yet laid to rest. Ten years ago, a plague swept across the Seven Kingdoms. Ten years ago, the Queen of Iomar's son was exiled and named the author of the magical plague. Now, in the present, Terrin works to complete his ultimate goal: Control of the Seven Kingdoms using his son's power to supplement his own. But his attempt at dominion meets resistance and the fate of the world rests in the unlikely hands of an exiled prince, a Dreamer, and a vampire...

Book 1: The Prince of Shadows

When Alban's father Terrin appeared at the castle door with a vampire in tow and apologies on his lips, Alban fell under his spell just like everyone else and welcomed him home. But Terrin didn't return to live quietly in his brother's kingdom. He had other plans and, with Alban's untrained powers at his disposal, he begins his ruthless plan to destroy the Seven Kingdoms and rule them all, beginning with his brother's death.

Terrin engineers events to cast the blame on his nephew, Teluride, intending to see the boy executed for his father's murder. But there are those who would thwart Terrin in his mad plan for power, and Alban forms an unlikely alliance with Skade, the reclusive Queen of Iomar, and Terrin's slave, a young vampire with no memory of his name or origins. Although the future looks grim, Alban and the vampire attempt to stop Terrin...and they almost succeed.

A darker history lies at the heart of Terrin's treachery, and only Skade knows the true reason why Terrin would murder his own brother and attempt to destroy both Alban and the vampire to achieve his goals. The Ghost who resides in Skade's mirror--her servant and thrall--holds one of the keys to Terrin's madness. Unfortunately, more than one person wishes for the past to remain the past and the future to hold no shadows of what might have been...

Publisher: http://www.writers-exchange.com/the-prince-of-shadows/

Book 2: Lost In Shadows

Events set in motion ten years ago come to a head as Skade, the reclusive Queen of Iomar, and Nicodemus, who is imprisoned by Skade, struggle to free Alban and the vampire from Terrin's grasp. Old secrets come to light when Skade's exiled son is forced to face his past--or die trying to redeem himself once and for all. Can the crimes of the past truly be forgiven? Only time will tell...and time is running out.

Publisher: http://www.writers-exchange.com/lost-in-shadows/

Book 3: Bound In Shadows

With his power crushed, brother to the king and father to Alban, Terrin is forced to take drastic measures to regain his sons after they are freed and harness the power they possess. But he has an ally inside the healer's house where they are recovering who works to further his plans. The Queen of Iomar, Skade's son, courts redemption to try to save his mother's life, and the vampire who no longer remembers his own name dreams a dream that might save them all...or damn them if success is thwarted.

Publisher: http://www.writers-exchange.com/bound-in-shadows/

A Beth-Hill Novel: Wild Hunt Series

Are creatures of the night and all manner of extramundane beings drawn to certain locations in the natural world? In the Midwestern village of Beth-Hill located in southern Ohio, the population is made up of its fair share of common citizens...and much more than its share of supernatural residents. Take a walk on the wild side in this unusual place where imagination meets reality.

The Wild Hunt roamed the forest outside of Beth-Hill until the Council bound them for a hundred years. Nevertheless, a century of existence has made an indelible mark not easily forgotten for these ghostly myths that are no longer so ghostly or myth-like...

Book 1: Heart's Desire

The Wild Hunt roamed the forest outside of Beth-Hill until the Council bound them for a hundred years--a lifetime for a human but only a passing thought to one such as Gabriel, Master of the Wild Hunt. As the Council's binding draws to a close, old enemies reappear to ensure that the Wild Hunt is bound once more--to a creature much worse than the Council has been.

Publisher: http://www.writers-exchange.com/hearts-desire/

Book 2: Fire and Water

As a young vampire, Erialas Morgan brought his mother back to life with a spell that shouldn't exist, shouldn't have worked...perhaps shouldn't have been performed at all. Desperation and love are his only excuses for doing the unthinkable.

There are others who wish to use that same spell for their own gain--and to destroy the Wild Hunt once and for all. Caught in the middle of a war between the Morgan clan of vampires and their human kin, Erialas turns to the Hunt for help. But even Gabriel, the Master of the Wild Hunt, may not be able to stop the tide of death and destruction once it turns.

Publisher: http://www.writers-exchange.com/fire-and-water/

Book 3: The Lost

Almost sixty years ago, Darkbrook, the only school of magic in the United States, opened its doors to students of decidedly different natures, sending out letters of invitation to the elves, the dragons, and the vampires. The three who responded to the invitation banded together despite their differences but vanished only weeks later along with an entire classroom full of students and their teacher after a field trip gone horribly wrong.

The Wild Hunt has healed and the Hounds have grown closer together, keeping Darkbrook's forest safe and secure for those who live there. Malachi, one of the eldest members of the Wild Hunt, has adapted to Josiah's spell to help him see, but when a demon boy trapped in the body of a human body for sixty years inside the school disrupts the newfound calm, the Hunt--and those they protect--are thrust into a struggle that should have ended long ago when a vampire, an elf, and a dragon vanished into the Mists.

Publisher: http://www.writers-exchange.com/the-lost/

Book 4: A Glint of Silver

Jericho is a vampire who wants is to live away from the Richmond household of vampires led by his ruthless father Connor. When Jericho tries to escape, Connor punishes him and leaves him to die. Tristan is determined to be the one to bring Jericho back, but he can't see him suffer for wanting a normal life. As long as Connor lives, Jericho will never be safe or free. As long as Connor *lives...*

Publisher: http://www.writers-exchange.com/a-glint-of-silver/

Book 5: All That Glitters

As a member of the cruel Morgan Household of vampires, twelve-year-old Arthur Morgan has been abused all his life.

Maya, a water fairy, shows him just how horrible and twisted the household he's grown up is. With her help, and the unexpected help of an adult vampire, Arthur attempts to escape.

Can he become something more than what his father has decreed?

Publisher: http://www.writers-exchange.com/all-that-glitters/

The Chelsea Chronicles

Normally a quiet, serene place, Chelsea Kingdom seems like the perfect location for a centuries' old vampire to blend in and live a normal life, even escape hunters and an angry mob. Unfortunately, his timing couldn't be worse...

Book 1: So You Want to be a Vampire

Chelsea Kingdom is usually a pretty quiet place but recent murders--committed by a vampire--upset the calm. Newcomer to town, Vlad Dhalgren wants only to blend in and live a normal life. He quickly learns that isn't possible, given that other vampires have been hiding in the shadows around the castle--in plain sight--for years.

Despite her lineage, Anna Everett, the crown princess of the Kingdom of Chelsea, isn't a wizard like her father, which means she will never be Queen. She has only one friend, Valerian Moreton--Val--who has secrets he's never shared that could get him *and* Anna killed...

Publisher: http://www.writers-exchange.com/so-you-want-to-be-a-vampire/

Book 2: Transformation

As Anna, crown princess of Chelsea, adjusts to life as a vampire after recent events, Vlad plans for a future he has no real hope to seeing come to pass due to injuries sustained while attempting to save Anna's life. But, as life goes on for Anna and her friend Valerian "Val" Moreton, it changes for others--some of whom are not quite what they seem...

Publisher: http://www.writers-exchange.com/transformation/

You can find ALL our books up on our website at:

http://www.writers-exchange.com

All Jennifer's books:

http://www.writers-exchange.com/Jennifer-St-Clair/

all our fantasy novels:

http://www.writers-exchange.com/category/genres/fantasy/

www.ingramcontent.com/pod-product-compliance
Lightning Source LLC
Chambersburg PA
CBHW071358130726
47996CB00002B/982